'Snooping again, Giana?'

Unseen, unheard, Breid Winterton had returned, and now his tall figure filled the doorway, standing between her and escape.

'I . . . you did say I could explore the house.'

'Why this room?' he asked. 'And what interest does that portrait hold for you?' He watched her intently.

'I'm . . . I'm a little like her,' she said hesitantly, afraid of giving offence, of presuming where the woman he'd loved was concerned.

'A *little* like her!' It was a growl of pain. 'My God! You're damnably like her—or as she was twenty years ago, when we were first married. In a way, having you here is almost like having her back.' He gave a grating laugh. 'It sounds ridiculous, doesn't it, at my age, playing games of pretend? But sometimes I've tried to imagine you *are* Francesca.' And, as Giana shifted uneasily, 'Oh don't worry,' his voice was harshly mocking. 'That's as far as it goes. I'm not asking you to stand in for her in any other sense of the word.'

DON'T
ASK WHY

BY

ANNABEL MURRAY

MILLS & BOON LIMITED
ETON HOUSE   18-24 PARADISE ROAD
RICHMOND   SURREY   TW9 1SR

First published in Great Britain 1988
by Mills & Boon Limited

© Annabel Murray 1988

Australian copyright 1988
Philippine copyright 1989
This edition 1989

ISBN 0 263 76197 5

Set in Times Roman 10 on 12¼ pt.
01-8901-51817 C

Made and printed in Great Britain

For Sheila Walsh
Friend and Mentor
with thanks

'Don't ask why, ask what for.'

Carl Jung

CHAPTER ONE

ON SUNDAY morning the watcher was still in the square. It was his third consecutive morning—surely too often for coincidence.

Giana stood slightly to one side of the bedroom window, her tall, slender figure concealed by heavy gold curtains. February could be a treacherous month and a flu-like cold which had run riot among her colleagues had kept her off work and indoors for several days. Now, as on the previous two mornings, she observed without being observed, her heart-shaped face with its high cheekbones set in serious lines.

Godolphin Buildings stood around an inner courtyard of fountains and rosebeds which in summer would be a blaze of colour. At the moment everything was a uniform grey. At each of the four corners an archway gave access to the busy London streets outside. It was in one of these archways that the watcher had taken up his position this morning, sheltered against the heavy rain. What was the man's interest in this block of flats?

Giana wasn't normally of a nervous disposition. Her work called for her to be fit, to have both physical and emotional stamina. But there was something unnerving in the man's unmoving stance and, oddly, he was making no attempt at concealment. There must be two hundred people living in Godolphin Buildings and it was idiotic of course to suppose that the watcher had any con-

nection with herself, or even with Anthony, who, in the
course of his work, must have made many enemies of
one sort or another. She'd meant to mention the watcher
to Anthony last night. But Anthony had arrived home
late from his current assignment, tired and bad-tempered,
as he often was these days.

She turned her head slightly to look at her husband
where he lay sprawled in the big double bed, as always
occupying more than his fair share of the space. Her
hazel eyes were troubled as she studied the round, bland
face that once she'd thought so handsome.

Giana wasn't quite sure when she'd first realised that
her year-old marriage to Anthony Leyburn had been a
mistake. Perhaps the knowledge had crept up on her
gradually as she'd come to know more about the virtual
stranger she'd married.

She returned her attention to the watcher. He was still
there. Impulsively she decided to get dressed and go out
and take a closer look at him. Her cold was in its last
throes. She would be able to go back to work tomorrow.
Suddenly she felt restless and cooped up, and Anthony
would sleep for hours yet. Besides, if the man on the
corner was some kind of villain it might be handy to be
able to give a detailed description of him.

Throughout the current winter Giana had taken to
wearing colourful tracksuits around the flat. Now it was
only the work of a moment to don her bright red mack-
intosh, matching rain hat and suitable shoes. In her mood
of energetic restlessness she disdained the lift and ran
lightly down the four flights of stairs.

It was still early and the courtyard was empty; Sunday
morning and the steadily falling rain were keeping other

residents indoors. At the outside door she paused, sudden doubt assailing her. Just suppose the watcher was waiting for *her*? Then she shrugged away the ridiculous notion and stepped out briskly in his direction.

As she approached him her keen brain assimilated and stored facts which might be useful. He was below average height, of indeterminate age but probably around fifty. Clean-shaven. Half-moon glasses. A jaunty spotted bowtie peeped between the revers of his coat—astrakhan to match his hat. He looked eccentric rather than alarming, and his expression remained uninterested as Giana strode past. Her challenging 'good morning', issued in her throaty, attractive voice, received the barest acknowledgement.

As she turned the corner of the street she glanced back. No one dogged her footsteps. And after two or three such checks she drew in a sigh of relief and was able to laugh at herself.

'Being cooped up indoors has made me quite neurotic,' she told a damp huddled pigeon.

She took the Underground and fifteen minutes later she was window-shopping on Oxford Street. When she returned to the flat, some two hours later, the watcher was still there, but this time she ignored him. Fresh air and exercise had restored her sense of proportion. There was probably some perfectly good reason for his presence in the square. She was even ready to cope with whatever mood Anthony produced when he awoke.

Surprisingly, it was an affable one. He was already up and dressed and preparing lunch, an uncommon occurrence.

'How was the trip?' Giana asked him as they ate.

'Extremely satisfactory,' he said smugly. 'I got a good story from the rapist's ex-girlfriend. It'll be on the front page tomorrow.'

Anthony was an investigative journalist for one of the more sensational dailies. Mostly he specialised in exposés of the famous, the wealthy and the influential. But occasionally he handled lurid crimes of violence. And though Giana did not like his work or his attitude towards the people he researched, she had to admit his pieces were well written.

He went on with some enthusiasm to relate the facts he had uncovered. When an assignment had gone well he was always on a high, even though the mood might not be of long duration. Today, Giana thought dispassionately, he seemed more excitedly febrile than usual. His swarthy features were animated, his dark eyes glittering. And in the next few moments she thought she knew why.

'Fancy a night out?' he asked with would-be-casualness. 'There's a do on at old Pratt's place tonight.'

Simon Pratt, the owner of the paper Anthony worked for, moved in exalted circles. One could always be certain of meeting the celebrated or the notorious at his parties. Anthony must be on the trail of another story, and it must be a big one to incite all this euphoria.

Sometimes, after a full week's work, Giana did not feel like attending these rather empty social occasions. And she knew it didn't matter to Anthony whether she went or not; he would go whatever happened. But she'd had several days of enforced inactivity and Anthony's mood had made her curious.

'Yes, all right,' she agreed.

This settled, Anthony went on talking. It was typical of him, Giana thought, that he didn't reciprocate by asking how *her* work had gone while he'd been away. Very early in their marriage she'd given up discussing the hospital or her patients with him. Perhaps because Anthony himself had come from a deprived working-class background, he mistrusted and denigrated the efforts of workers in the public sector. If he were ever to need hospitalisation, she reflected, he would make an awful patient, the kind nurses dreaded.

Both Giana and her husband had got where they were by their own industry.

Giana had left school after her 'O' Levels. Her father, vicar of a small parish in Hertfordshire, couldn't afford to keep her in full-time education for another two years. She had done shorthand and typing at school and at first she'd been employed as a secretary-cum-ancillary worker in a residential establishment for the mentally handicapped, not far from her Hertfordshire home. She had liked the work but decided that being a secretary did not totally satisfy her ambitions or her need to help others. On attaining her eighteenth birthday she had applied and been accepted for training as a nurse. Three years later she was a fully qualified SRN and since her marriage had obtained a post in a London hospital.

She had met Anthony Leyburn at a party to which a friend had dragged her. It was not the kind of party Giana normally attended, though she'd realised since that such events were meat and drink to Anthony. It was a sophisticated affair, the conversation and acquaintance superficial, and Giana had felt very much out of her depth. It was surprising now to recollect how Anthony had come to her rescue. It had honestly never occurred to the modest Giana that her striking looks far outweighed her obvious lack of importance. When the party was over they had left together. Attracted to him, she had agreed to see him again. Their friendship ripened and soon Giana believed herself to be in love.

Her parents disapproved of her involvement with Anthony. They were not harsh or censorious. It was more of an unease that they expressed.

'He's too old for you...' Anthony was eleven years older than Giana. '...and he's not our sort,' her mother had warned. 'And I don't mean because he comes from a poor background. God forbid I should indulge in such snobbery, especially in our circumstances. But, Giana, your father's had several long talks with him. Anthony just doesn't have the same values, the sense of responsibility we've tried to teach you. There's a hard, rather callous streak about him. And you don't seem to have anything in common. That's a very important element in a marriage, darling, it really is.'

But Giana had thought she knew best. Anthony was fun. He made her laugh. He still could. And nowadays she often felt guilty because she didn't love him as much as he must love her.

It didn't take Giana long to decide what to wear that evening. Though Anthony now commanded a good salary, she'd insisted that while they were both working she would pay her own way, and she did not possess a vast wardrobe. She had job security and sometimes job satisfaction, but the career prospects and pay were hardly inspiring.

The simply cut black dress always looked good on her tall, slender figure, making the ash-blonde fairness of her hair seem even lighter by comparison. The barest touch of make-up that was all her good complexion ever needed, and the few pieces of jewellery she owned completed her outfit.

They took a taxi to the Pratts'. The party was already in full swing when they arrived. Simon Pratt was surrounded by two or three drinking cronies, but his wife Fay came to greet them.

'Georgiana!' Fay always gave Giana her full name, 'How nice. You don't often come to see us.'

Giana liked the older woman. Unlike her burly boisterous husband, Fay Pratt was small and thin with a quiet, faded manner.

Predictably, Anthony disappeared at once and Fay led the way to the cloakroom where Giana left her modest coat among the assorted fur wraps hanging there.

'I suspect,' Fay went on as they returned to the large drawing-room, 'like me, you don't much care for these dos?'

'I'm sure you give very nice parties,' Giana said hastily, anxious not to offend her hostess, 'but I'm usually whacked at weekends. All I want to do is flop and get my feet up.'

'And get away from people?' the other woman hazarded shrewdly. 'Besides, I imagine you find the sort you meet here much less worthwhile than those you encounter in the course of your work?'

'I don't find I have much in common with these people,' Giana agreed with a nod towards the crowded room. 'It doesn't seem right that some people should have so little and others so much. Not that I've any Communist leanings,' she added, 'but I would like to see a fairer distribution of wealth and—particularly—health!'

A hovering waiter offered them cocktails and, as they sipped, Giana looked around her. As she'd anticipated, there were several well-known faces present and she wondered which of them was currently exciting Anthony's attention.

'Your husband's over there,' Fay Pratt pointed out. 'Such a handsome man, and so charming.'

'Yes,' Giana said drily.

Anthony had a bold approach, a charm that never failed to captivate strangers, women in particular. He could make a woman think she was the only person in the room who mattered. But Giana, who knew him better, was aware that every ingredient of that charm had been tested and perfected. She knew all his little tricks. The firm handclasp. The easy joke. The deep, deceptive candour of his gaze.

'Did you want to join him?' Fay asked.

'No, thanks. He won't want me around while he's grilling someone.' They both smiled at Giana's description of journalistic techniques.

The someone this time was a young brunette—very young. Giana didn't recognise her, though she must be of some importance to attract Anthony's notice. From his intent manner, he was subjecting her to some close questioning. Yes, she had to be business, Giana decided. She wasn't the type he usually flirted with. Anthony preferred mature, experienced women who knew the rules of the game, not the *ingénue* type who might take him seriously.

The two women found themselves a seat on a deep settee in an alcove and settled down to chat. Fay Pratt was genuinely interested in Giana's career.

'Are you still enjoying your work, Georgiana?'

Giana wrinkled her shapely nose attractively.

'I wouldn't say "enjoying" was exactly the word. It's not a glamour job, is it? But it is a challenging one and I'm doing what I wanted to do, helping people. But there are bad moments, too—when patients die in spite of everyone's efforts. And it's even worse when it's a young child that dies. That's the sad side of the work.'

'The part I should dislike the most is emptying bedpans,' Fay confessed. 'Or seeing accident cases brought in. Blood!' She shuddered. 'How do you stand it?'

'I don't think I'm particularly squeamish, though once or twice I have felt bad,' Giana admitted. 'But I try not to show it, of course. And so far I've managed not to panic when we've had a sudden rush of accident victims.' In fact Giana did herself less than justice. She had remained calm and clear-thinking throughout many a crisis. 'When people are badly hurt there isn't time to worry about yourself and how you feel.'

'Well I think you do a marvellous job,' Fay said warmly, 'It's a great pity nurses aren't better paid for what they have to do. How you cope with it I can't imagine. Shifts—evenings, nights, even weekends—*and* being a housewife!' Fay's life was totally devoted to her newspaper-tycoon husband's comfort, and Giana smiled at her emphatic manner.

Talking to Fay made the evening pass surprisingly quickly, even though it was well into the small hours before the first guest made to leave.

Anthony, Giana noticed, had spent almost the entire evening with the young woman, who was also extremely pretty.

'Who's the brunette in the yellow dress?' she asked Fay.

'No idea, except that I heard someone call her Tina. I don't know half the people who come to these affairs. Simon just tells me how many to cater for. Would you like me to ask Simon who she is?'

'Goodness, no. It's not important.' Giana hadn't been deliberately watching her husband. In the early days of their marriage she *had* been a little jealous when he'd paid attention to other women, but now she knew it was all a calculated part of his stock in trade. In public he was all affability and charm to those they met. In private he hadn't a good word to say for anyone, not even their mutual friends. His work, too, reflected his cynical attitude towards life and people in general.

Above all else, Giana prized sincerity. Perhaps it had been when she'd realised Anthony did not possess this quality that the disenchantment had begun and gradually she'd fallen out of love with her husband. If it had ever been love. Sometimes she wondered if it hadn't just been infatuation. Her parents had gently suggested that it might be.

Not that there was anything she could do about the unsatisfactory state of her marriage, Giana thought sadly. She had made her bed and she must lie on it—literally. There was no way she was going to let Anthony down. They might not be compatible, but he'd given her no other grounds for complaint. Besides, with her parents she'd had a secure and stable family existence in which codes of honour and unspoken rules existed. She still lived her life by those strong moral standards and believed staunchly in the sanctity of the marriage vows she'd taken. Her parents had been unhappy about her marriage but they would be shocked to the core if she left her husband. Divorce was something that happened to other people, the kind of people Anthony wrote about. Yet sometimes, on the rare occasions she allowed herself to dwell on it, the thought of the long years ahead dismayed and depressed her.

Maybe if she could have had a child things would have been different. But Anthony didn't want children.

'My mother had ten of us,' he'd told Giana once, 'and we lived in abject poverty. I'm not going to work my guts out to support a load of kids. In the end they don't thank you for it.'

Anthony was still cock-a-hoop on the journey home, though his conversation was all small talk. He never divulged anything about his current investigation until it was 'in the bag' as he put it. As usual he'd had plenty to drink, and Giana was glad they'd taken a taxi.

As the vehicle deposited them at the archway most convenient for their flat, Giana noticed another taxi overtake and draw up a few yards ahead of them. While Anthony paid their driver, she watched the occupant of the other taxi descend. It was the man in the astrakhan coat. She nudged Anthony.

'See that man?'

'What about him?'

'He's been hanging around here for several days. I believe he's watching someone. And he's just got out of that taxi. Suppose it's us he's following?'

'The chap probably lives here.'

'If he lives here, why would he stand around for hours in the rain, just watching the place?' Giana argued. 'Anthony, he makes me nervous.'

Rain was falling again and irritably Anthony hustled her inside the building.

'I don't see why. You're getting neurotic,' he told her. 'He's hardly likely to be after you.'

'I am *not* neurotic!' She refuted the suggestion indignantly. 'Besides,' she reminded him, 'he could equally well be watching you.'

'Most unlikely. Even if he were, he's only a pint-sized looking article. I can take care of myself.'

The bedside clock said almost half past three as they undressed, in silence for the most part. Giana could tell Anthony was still engrossed with thoughts of his latest project. From time to time a self-satisfied little smile curled his rather sensual mouth. Once in bed he gave Giana a perfunctory kiss, then almost immediately he fell asleep. He'd done that quite often in the last two or three months, and Giana was ashamed of her relief. Her husband had always been a highly sexual man and his recent abstention puzzled her. Sometimes she wondered if he was seeing another woman.

Not surprisingly, they both overslept next morning. For Anthony it wasn't such a disastrous occurrence, since his hours were flexible. Journalism wasn't a nine-till-five job, he'd told Giana in the early days of their marriage, when he'd been late for meals.

Neither was hers, Giana thought ruefully as she dressed hurriedly in her uniform, but she'd given up expecting Anthony to sympathise.

Anthony was the first to leave. As she dumped the breakfast pots in the sink to be washed that evening, a slovenly necessity she deplored, Giana watched him stride across the courtyard below. Although they had a car, Anthony only used it when a story took him out of the city.

She was in a hurry, but for some reason she loitered to watch him out of sight. Suddenly she stiffened. Casually, but none the less certainly for all that, the watcher was following her husband.

She snatched up coat and handbag and flew downstairs, but when she emerged into the square both men were out of sight. She knew the route Anthony took every morning. Forgetting for the moment that she was late and that she was going in the opposite direction from the bus she normally caught, she plunged into the Underground and struggled through the thronging commuters.

She reached the barrier too late. Anthony was just disappearing down the escalator with his pursuer only yards behind him. She called his name, knowing even as she did so that it was useless.

She was fifteen minutes late for work. She had thought of phoning Anthony at his office, to warn him that he'd been followed. But she knew he would probably scoff at her 'vivid imagination'. Besides, they were short staffed on the ward. Most of the nurses were doing the work of two.

*   *   *

Her shift over, Giana still had errands to do before she could return home. These included visiting an elderly friend, something she tried to do at least two or three times a month. Old Mrs Hibbs was a former long-stay patient whom Giana had befriended. Quite often, with some patients, a strong bond was formed. But somehow Mrs Hibbs wasn't just 'a case'. She was special. In a way she reminded Giana of her late grandmother. Mrs Hibbs had no close relatives but, though she lived alone and was plagued by endless ailments, she was a cheerful soul who looked forward eagerly to Giana's visits.

'You look tired, dear,' was Mrs Hibbs' greeting.

'It's been a hectic day,' Giana said as she carried the tea tray through to the 'best room'.

'You try to do too much for other folks,' Mrs Hibbs said. 'Wonderful, you are. Next thing to a saint, and I'm a selfish old woman expecting you to call on me like you do.'

'Nonsense!' Giana smiled. 'Coming to see you relaxes me, helps me unwind before I go home. So I don't take out the day's frustrations on my husband,' she joked.

But despite her fatigue and the depression which sometimes overtook her at the end of the day, she listened quietly as Mrs Hibbs chattered on. She'd heard all the old lady's stories before, but Mrs Hibbs had very few visitors, sometimes none between Giana's calls. Part of the ritual was that they should listen to the news together. Mrs Hibbs wouldn't have a television in the house.

'Give me the radio any day,' she said as she always did. 'Leaves more room for the imagination.'

The period while the news was on was the only time Mrs Hibbs ceased her flow of conversation and Giana was able to relax her attention. She leaned back and closed her eyes, letting the reader's soothing tones wash over her. She was vaguely aware that he was reporting on the usual worldwide disasters: wars, rumours of wars. And there were problems at a national level: only that afternoon an aeroplane on a charter flight had nose-dived into the Channel with probable loss of lives. There had been a motorway pile-up in the north of England, due to thick fog.

But she wasn't giving the broadcast her full attention. Her mind was still half on a family she'd talked to earlier at the hospital and to whom she'd had to break the news of their tragic bereavement. Listening to other people's depression ought to make you count your own blessings, Giana thought. But sometimes she felt just like a sponge for other people's misery, and the anguish she absorbed seemed to stay with her for hours. Her colleagues told her she let herself become too involved, but somehow she just couldn't help people by remaining a detached observer on the edge of their sorrow. Her train of thought continued as she wondered if there was anything she'd left undone or unsaid that could have helped that family.

'Terrible, isn't it?' The old lady leaned forward and switched off the radio, and guiltily Giana snapped out of her introspective mood. 'All those people missing. Their poor relatives.' Then, with a prosaicness that restored everyday sanity, 'Another cup of tea, dear? Another scone?'

'No, thanks, Mrs Hibbs.' Regretfully, 'I really ought to be going.'

'Not yourself today, are you?' the old lady commented. 'You're usually so bright and cheerful. A lovely-looking girl like you should always be smiling. You wouldn't think it to look at me now, but I once had lovely silvery-blonde hair like yours.' She hobbled ahead of Giana to open the door. 'See you again soon?' she asked anxiously.

'I hope so.' Giana bent and kissed the soft elderly cheek.

There was still her shopping to be done at the late-night supermarket. Then there was a long queue for the bus and when it came it was crowded, standing room only. Giana was thankful to reach her stop. She was tired, but nevertheless she hurried along the street, threading her way in and out of the crowds, the heavily laden carrier bags bumping against her long slender legs. It was a relief to find there was no watcher on the corner tonight.

She took the lift to the top floor, unlocked her front door and set down her shopping with a thankful sigh. Though she was later than usual, she was still first home. Thank goodness. Anthony disliked being kept waiting for his evening meal. She unpacked the shopping and began to prepare dinner. While it cooked she showered and changed out of her workaday uniform into one of her casual leisure suits. She might even have time for a much needed cup of coffee. She didn't really like tea, but she'd never had the heart to tell Mrs Hibbs so.

She switched on the television just in time for the news. It was almost word for word what she'd heard on the radio. She flicked to another channel, swung her feet up on to the settee and sipped her coffee as she watched.

It was the dregs of her drink soaking through her trousers that woke Giana to the realisation that she'd been dozing for at least half an hour and her cup had upended itself. Heavens! The dinner! Fortunately it was a casserole and it hadn't spoilt. But still no Anthony? If he was going to be this late he usually tried to get to a phone and let her know. She looked out of the window. The square below was empty, dark except for the lamp-post at each corner. No one loitered in any of the archways. Giana's earlier nervousness returned. No watcher and no Anthony. The two facts assumed a sinister significance.

Then she saw the note which, earlier, her tired eyes had failed to see. It had slipped down and lay flat on top of the television set. She ripped open the envelope. 'Came back to pack a case,' the message read. 'Following up a promising lead. Expect me when you see me.' Giana heaved a sigh of relief. Her imagination *had* been working overtime.

It was part of Anthony's rebellion against his deprived youth that he demanded everything be done in style. But with no need this evening to make an effort, Giana served her own dinner on a tray in front of the television, and after watching a couple of favourite programmes she washed up and decided on an early night.

The rest of the week passed in uneventful routine. There were no further communications from Anthony, but that wasn't unusual when he was hot on the scent of a story.

On Friday, Giana was home early for once. As she got off the bus she saw the man in the astrakhan coat just leaving Godolphin Buildings. He couldn't have seen her, and on a sudden impulse she determined that *she* would follow *him*. It was surprisingly easy in the crowded

Underground to keep him in view while remaining unobserved herself. At Bond Street he left the train, walked briskly down a side street and entered an office block in a mews behind Claridges Hotel.

After a discreet interval Giana ventured into the foyer, where she discovered that two firms occupied the building: an estate agent downstairs and upstairs a firm of private investigators—Ellis and Palmer.

'Can I help you?'

Startled, Giana swung on her heel. She hadn't noticed anyone in the reception area. For a moment she stared at the smartly dressed girl, then her brain clicked into gear.

'That gentleman in the astrakhan coat, who just went upstairs. Was that Mr Palmer?'

'No, Mr Ellis. He's the senior partner. Did you want to see Mr Palmer? I'm afraid you'll need an appointment.'

'Er, no, thank you. I just...'

'Excuse me!' the receptionist said as her intercom system buzzed loudly. She flicked over a switch. 'Yes, Mr Ellis?'

'Miss Chisholm, I want the Anthony Leyburn report typed up right away and delivered to Mr Winterton's house this evening. I'd like you to attend to it personally, if you please.'

'Right you are, Mr Ellis.' The girl grimaced at Giana, who despite the confirmation of her suspicions was still a little stunned at hearing Anthony's name actually mentioned. 'That means overtime—again. It'll be the third time this week I've had to stand my boyfriend up.'

She picked up a notebook and pencil. 'Did you want an appointment with Mr Palmer?'

'Oh! No! It doesn't matter,' Giana said quickly. 'I'll leave it for now.'

She was getting quite adept at 'tailing' people, Giana thought complacently just over an hour later. She smiled. Maybe she should ask Ellis and Palmer for a job! But she sobered quickly. This wasn't a game; this was in earnest. Anthony was in some kind of trouble and she meant to find out who this Mr Winterton was.

Despite the cold she had hung about on the corner of the mews until the neat Miss Chisholm emerged from the office block and walked briskly to the Underground. There had been a considerable amount of changing trains and now they were on the outskirts of the city, an area Giana didn't know. But it was quite obviously expensively residential.

The quiet tree-lined street consisted of a long row of Georgian houses beautifully restored and maintained. Some bore the brass plates of professional men. As Miss Chisholm mounted the front steps of one of the houses Giana drew back out of sight behind one of the ancient trees. The other woman pushed a bulky envelope through the brass letterbox, descended the steps and began to retrace her steps. Hastily Giana turned her back and crossed the street, pretending interest in a dentist's nameplate.

In the hushed evening stillness of the residential area it was easy to hear when the click of high heels finally receded. Giana abandoned her study of the dentist's surgery hours and walked purposefully towards her goal.

In the brief interval she had decided what she was going to do. Boldly she mounted the steps and pressed the gleaming doorbell.

A trim maidservant opened the door and looked enquiringly at her. Giana took a deep breath.

'I've just delivered a letter for Mr Winterton. I put it through the letterbox, but then I thought perhaps I should have handed it to him personally, to make sure. It's very important.'

'Oh, dear! Is it?' The girl looked perturbed. 'Does it need an answer straight away? You see, Mr Winterton isn't here. He's gone down to the cottage.'

'The cottage?'

'Yes, Foxdene it's called, at Dinas Mead,' the girl went on, and Giana thanked her lucky stars this Mr Winterton didn't keep a manservant. They were usually more close-mouthed. 'Well, they call it the cottage, but it isn't really. Mr Winterton goes there a lot. We don't see much of him in town. Proper waste I call it, having this lovely house and hardly living in it. Doesn't seem right, does it, miss, when some folks have no home at all?'

Well that appeared to be that, Giana thought as she walked away. The maidservant had assured her the important letter would be sent on to Mr Winterton the very next day. But at least Anthony would have to believe her now. When he returned from his latest assignment she'd be able to tell him the name of the man who was having him followed.

But Anthony didn't return. Or at least, after ten days he was still away and she'd received no message from him. He wasn't usually gone this long without some kind of communication, and Giana was worried. Yet she hesitated to make enquiries. She had only ever phoned his office once when he'd been late home and he'd been very annoyed. He had told her he didn't want her checking up on him. But that had been only a matter of hours. Surely this was different. Finally, one evening, still in a quandary, she telephoned Fay Pratt.

The older woman was immediately concerned and helpful.

'I'll talk to Simon right away. He prides himself on having his finger on every pulse. And if he doesn't know what assignment Anthony's on and where to contact him, he'll know just who to ask. Try not to worry, Georgiana. I'm sure Anthony's perfectly all right. You know what these men are when there's a good story to be had. They forget all about us.'

A couple of hours later Fay called back and Giana was no wiser but considerably more concerned. As far as Simon Pratt and his chief editor knew, Anthony Leyburn had not been assigned to any story. In fact, the office staff were under the impression that he was on holiday.

'Do you think you ought to tell the police he's missing?' Fay asked.

Giana considered this but rejected the idea. As one of the newspaper's senior reporters there was just a chance that, as he'd done once or twice before, Anthony had gone off on his own initiative. He would be furious if she set up a hue and cry for him, broke his cover and ruined something he was working on.

On the other hand she couldn't stand idly by and just assume that Anthony would return safely. If he was in trouble of some kind she'd never be able to forgive herself. She must do *something*. It was only a hunch but, having nowhere else to begin, she decided to start with the mysterious Mr Winterton.

She was rather surprised to find that he was not too mysterious to be listed in the telephone directory—B Winterton, 27 Makepeace Gardens, London E3. She planned carefully what she would say. She wouldn't ask to speak to him. That might draw a straight refusal. She would simply ask if he was back from—where was it?—oh, yes, Dinas Mead.

No, Mr Winterton was still away, a man's voice told her—so there was a manservant—but she declined to leave a message.

It was fortunate that Anthony hadn't needed the car, Giana thought a few days later as she drove out of London. Remembering the ubiquitous Mr Ellis, she'd taken elaborate precautions about her departure, leaving home in the early hours of the morning. But she hadn't made any forward plans. At this time of year there shouldn't be any difficulty about accommodation. Giana had four weeks' holiday owing to her and she'd decided she was going down to Kent, to Dinas Mead, to see what she could find out about this Mr Winterton and—maybe—his connection with her husband.

As daylight woke the countryside she saw that her route passed still barren hop gardens and rough copses with glimpses of the immense Weald of Kent to the east. She'd had no sleep before she set out, and as she drove she flicked the car radio from station to station in search of something entertaining to keep her attention alert. There wasn't much choice. Jangling pop music or news broadcasts. She settled for the news. As usual there was nothing good about it. Politicians spent their time in slanging matches instead of sorting out the country's problems. Another war had begun in the Middle East. Some bodies had been recovered from the recent aeroplane crash; others were still missing. Sighing, she decided to put up with the pop music.

At midday, after a break, she reached her objective.

Dinas Mead was very much off the beaten track. It consisted of a cluster of cottages, a pub and a general store cum post office set around a common, too small ever to draw a crowd, merely an expanse of gorse and thorn pierced by grassy paths. It didn't even have the traditional village pond. In summer it would probably be a charming place but on this late February morning drenched by rain it was a dismal enough spot.

Giana left her car outside the Cock and Bull and strolled around the circumference of the green. The cottages were all named—Ivy Thatch, Primrose Cottage, etc, but there was no Foxdene. Baffled, she retraced her steps to the shop, surely a certain source of information.

'Foxdene?' the postmistress said. 'Yes, that's Mr Winterton's place, up above. Take the lane by the church. It's about half a mile, you can't miss it. You'll be here about the job, I suppose? Terrible trouble Mr Winterton has keeping his secretaries. They don't like it hereabouts in winter. No night life, d'you see?'

She seemed blessed by gossipy women, Giana thought exultantly. Now she had a cast-iron excuse for actually confronting Winterton.

'What's he like?' she asked, feigning nervousness. 'To work for, I mean?'

'I can't say, dear, never having been in that position. But he's pleasant enough when he comes in here. Pleasant, but not forthcoming. Likes to keep himself to himself, does Mr Winterton. A bit of a mystery. They do say,' she leant forward confidentially across the counter, 'that there's been some dreadful tragedy in his life, made him turn inwards, like.'

A customer entered the shop and the postmistress excused herself. Giana made her way back to her car. She debated whether to go into the Cock and Bull for a meal and perhaps pick up some further gossip about her quarry, or whether she should go straight on to Foxdene. Curiosity and eagerness to reach her goal made her decide on the latter course of action.

By the church the road turned right, entering tall woods of ash and oak, and emerged in a steep lane, at the top of which an open gate bore the name 'Foxdene'. Giana drove through the gateway, up the winding drive and braked in front of the house. Its own woods shut it away from the road and from the village below. As Winterton's maidservant had said, it wasn't a cottage but an old, timbered manor house with richly moulded plaster coatings and brick mullioned windows. For a moment or two she sat looking at the house, mustering up her courage. A last-minute thought made her take the precaution of removing her wedding ring.

'Well, here goes!' Giana muttered as she tugged the old-fashioned bellpull.

A second and a third attempt failed to elicit any answer, and Giana stared up in frustration at the enigmatic windows. It seemed the mysterious Mr Winterton was out. She supposed she could go back to the pub, book a room and return later. But the idea dissatisfied her. There was nothing to stop her making a tour of the outside of the building and this she did, stopping occasionally to peer in through the ground-floor windows. Mr Winterton certainly did himself well, judging by the antique furnishings.

At the rear of the house a long garden ended in a shrubbery backed by yet more woodland. The entire ground-floor wall was flanked by a glass conservatory— and the outside door opened to her touch. Giana walked in and looked about her. The building was centrally heated and there were a great many lush tropical-looking plants. Giana didn't know much about gardening. As a child she hadn't been interested, and now living in a flat didn't present any opportunity for learning. But she did know that hothouse plants disliked draughts. She closed the door again before making her way through the conservatory, but hesitated on the threshold of the house itself.

'Who the hell are you? And how did you get in?'

The room was nearly as dark as the weather outside and she hadn't seen the man sitting in the swivel leather chair. He rose and, without taking his eyes off Giana, in one swift stride he moved and snapped on an overhead light.

'Good God!' For a moment he seemed totally stunned, his face drawn into lines of shock, almost as if she'd been a ghost, Giana thought. Then, 'Who are you?' He had a deep, beautiful voice. 'I warn you, reporters get short shrift here—male *or* female.'

'I'm not a reporter!' Giana stared bemusedly at him as she made the denial.

He was tall—six foot plus—and lean. His thin, intelligent face was also exceedingly handsome. His hair was blond but silvered with grey. He pleased her eyes, she realised with a kind of dismay. He had the sort of good looks that she'd thought existed only in library books on the shelves marked 'Romance'. But he was the villain, not the hero, she reminded herself.

'Prove you're not a reporter!' he snapped.

Giana extended her arms wide, her hazel eyes frankly ingenuous.

'Look, no notebook, no tape recorder, no camera.'

'But you know how reporters operate,' he retorted.

'I'm not ignorant. I dare say I could describe the hallmarks of various professions for you.'

'All right! So you're not a reporter—maybe.' Then, without any lessening of suspicion in his voice, 'What *do* you claim to be and what are you doing creeping about my house?'

'I rang the bell, three times. I thought it might not be working.'

'It's working.' His tone was grim. 'But I chose not to answer it.'

'Then you've only yourself to blame,' Giana told him, 'that I had to come round the back.'

'Had to?' he emphasised. Thick, straight eyebrows lifted ironically.

'If I wanted to see you.'

'And why should you want to see me?'

'You *are* Mr Winterton? You're looking for a secretary, aren't you?'

'I'm Breid Winterton, yes,' he admitted. 'But how do you know I need a secretary? I haven't advertised.'

'I found out at the post office.'

'Really?' He was sarcastic. 'I haven't sunk yet to the level of putting postcards in shop doorways.'

'The postmistress told me. She said you have difficulty keeping your secretaries. I'm beginning to see why,' Giana concluded pointedly.

'So I need a secretary and you just happen to be passing my doorstep? How convenient!'

Giana shrugged. She felt suddenly exhausted and dispirited. It had been a long day.

'That's the way it is. I'm between jobs and I decided to explore Kent. Believe it or not, as you like.'

'I don't believe it...' he began, but as he spoke he took a step towards her in what Giana construed as a threatening gesture. Instinctively she flinched, and suddenly everything went black as she collapsed in an undignified heap at his feet.

CHAPTER TWO

'WHEN did you last eat?'

As Giana's eyelids fluttered open, Breid Winterton's deep voice rapped out the question, but he sounded concerned rather than angry.

Giana had to think before she answered. She'd stopped once en route that morning for a coffee. But apart from that...

'Last night,' she confessed.

'Good God! No wonder you threw a wobbley on me. Stay right where you are,' he commanded. 'Don't move. I won't be long.'

She was stretched out full-length on a leather chesterfield, she discovered, and despite his admonition, as his tall figure disappeared through the door, Giana swung her feet to the floor and pulled down her sweater, which must have ridden up when he'd scooped her off the floor. She straightened her woollen skirt which was showing far too much of her shapely legs, pushed her long fair hair back from her face and wished she hadn't left her handbag in the car. Goodness, she must look a mess, travel-creased and weary, her make-up non-existent.

In his absence she took the opportunity to look around her. This room was furnished, not with antiques, but as an office, comfortable but functional. A long desk held a system which she recognised as a popular word processor. She'd used one just like it at the residential home.

There were three enormous filing cabinets. Row upon row of books dominated one wall but she dared not move to look at them. She wasn't sure she could trust her legs yet.

She'd never fainted before in her life, and Breid Winterton was probably right. Her collapse had been due to lack of food. But nerves, too, had played their part; she hadn't known what she might be walking into when she'd come to Foxdene. Though oddly, now she had met the mysterious Mr Winterton, he didn't frighten her. True, she had been wary and on the defensive, but there had been an element of enjoyment, a tingling, challenging excitement in their swift repartee.

Breid Winterton was as good as his word. He was back in five minutes with a plate of inelegantly chunky sandwiches and a mug of coffee. He apologised ruefully for their lack of daintiness.

'I'm afraid it's my housekeeper's day off.'

'They're very good,' Giana assured him as her straight white teeth bit into the crunchy salad filling. 'I hadn't realised how hungry I was.' Her naturally husky voice deepened as she told him, 'I'm sorry to be such a nuisance.'

'No problem,' he assured her. He perched on one arm of the chesterfield. Seated, the taut fabric of his jeans emphasised the line of his lower body and thighs and hastily Giana averted her eyes. 'Times are hard, eh?' he asked sympathetically. 'Been out of work long?'

His eyes, which she'd noticed were a shade somewhere between grey and blue, subjected her slender figure and heart-shaped high-cheeked face to a comprehensive survey.

Giana felt herself beginning to blush, not because of his appraisal but because she realised he thought she hadn't eaten because she was hard up, and because she knew she wasn't going to disabuse him of that idea. Not if it meant he'd give her a job as his secretary. He wasn't to know she could only stay a month—the duration of her leave. Surely in that time she'd be able to discover why he was having Anthony followed.

'Can you supply references?' he asked, breaking in on her reverie.

She nodded. But despite her determined course of action he was going a little fast for Giana. Not a man to beat about the bush, this Breid Winterton. Nor was he anybody's fool, she suspected. She would have to tread warily.

There was no problem about a reference; the home for the handicapped would confirm her secretarial capabilities. They didn't know she'd married since leaving them, so they wouldn't be surprised if she applied for a reference under her former name. She certainly couldn't give Breid Winterton her married name, she thought wryly.

'I'm not making any promises, mind! But if I'm satisfied with their account of you, I'll give you a trial.'

'What do you do?' she asked him.

'I write,' he said shortly. 'But hadn't we better introduce ourselves properly if you're going to work for me?' He held out his hand. 'Breid Winterton. And you're...?'

A brief hesitation and then she put her hand into his. His was a nice hand, strong and capable-looking with well kept fingernails. The back of his hand and his wrist where it emerged from the cuff of his shirtsleeve were both covered with a fine mat of blond hair that looked sensuously soft. The hand was nice to touch, too, warm and dry with a strong grip. She disliked limp hand-shakes. Then she realised her hand still lay in his and hastily removed it.

'Giana—short for Georgiana—Giana Spencer. But do you mean you're going to give me the job, just like that,' she said incredulously, 'without knowing any more about me?'

'I need a secretary,' he said simply. 'I'm willing to give you a month's trial. And we'll have plenty of time to get to know each other. I'm afraid I don't work conventional office hours. When I want to dictate I'll expect you to be available at any time.'

'Not at night, I hope?' she said, then flushed, hoping he wouldn't misconstrue her meaning.

He didn't. But he knew she was aware of the danger of *double entendre* for he smiled rather grimly.

'No,' he agreed. 'The night-time hours will be strictly your own. Now, accommodation. You've no objection to living in?' And, as she hesitated, 'My housekeeper does, so you've no need to worry about the proprieties.' His next words took Giana's breath away, made her hazel eyes widen. 'When could you start? Tomorrow?'

'But my references, surely you'll want to take those up first? And I've only got a small suitcase with me. I'd have to...'

'There's a rather useful invention known as the telephone,' he reminded her. 'Give me the number of your previous employer. And surely you've a friend who could pack up what you need for now and send it on to you?'

'Yes, but . . .'

'Right,' briskly. 'That's settled.' He stood up. 'We'd better see about a room for you. Where's your luggage? At the Cock and Bull? If so . . .'

'No, it's outside, in my car.'

'You can still afford to run a car?' For a moment the old suspicious look was back on his handsome face. Then he relaxed. 'Well I suppose we've all got pet things we'd hang on to in similar circumstances. Different people, different priorities. Give me your keys and I'll bring your stuff in.'

Bemusedly, Giana obeyed and as he left the room once more she looked at her wristwatch. She'd been at Foxdene precisely twenty minutes and in that time she'd assumed a false identity and secured herself a live-in job as Breid Winterton's secretary. Some going, she applauded herself. Not that her self-satisfaction was totally unalloyed. She did deplore the necessity for deception. But then Breid Winterton's behaviour smacked of the underhand, setting his spies to dog Anthony's footsteps, she thought indignantly.

Things continued to move apace. In another ten minutes Breid had telephoned the residential home and appeared satisfied with their verbal report of her, which they'd promised to confirm in writing. She was glad when he left her alone to call Fay Pratt. It would have been very difficult to give Fay a satisfactorily convincing explanation with him listening in. As it was Fay sounded incredulous.

'You're having a holiday? When Anthony's missing? But . . .'

'I know it must seem odd.' Giana darted nervous glances towards the closed door as she spoke in a low voice. 'But we could all be mistaken. He might be on some very hush-hush assignment. He'd be annoyed if we called attention to him by going to the police.'

'Giana, are you sure you're all right? You sound very odd, and I can hardly make out what you're saying.'

'Yes, I'm fine. It must be a bad line. But I couldn't wait it out at the flat, Fay. I thought a change of scenery would help to pass the time till Anthony shows up again. If I send you the key to the flat and a list, could you pack up a few things and send them to a poste restante address for me?'

'Of course, dear.' But Fay still sounded doubtful, 'I suppose you know best. Will you be keeping in touch?'

'Of course. I'll ring the flat every evening in case Anthony turns up. And I'll ring you from time to time in case you hear anything.'

'Wouldn't it be best if you gave me your number?'

'Oh, no,' Giana said hastily. She didn't want Fay ringing here and asking to speak to Mrs Leyburn. 'I'll be touring around,' she improvised. 'I may not stay in one place for long.'

The room to which Breid Winterton showed her was quaintly attractive with white roughcast walls and low, beamed ceilings. The apricot-coloured curtains and soft furnishings were bright, chintzy and feminine. Somehow Giana didn't think Breid had chosen them.

'Feel free to look around the rest of the house,' he told her as he left her to unpack. 'I'll be in the office for the next few hours if you want me. I'm afraid we'll have to eat out this evening—at the Cock and Bull. Seven o'clock suit you? I'd ask you to rustle something up for us, but I'm afraid Mrs Pimblett is a bit possessive about her domain.'

Which was handy, Giana thought when she was on her own once more. It would give her an opportunity to see how the inhabitants of Dinas Mead treated Breid Winterton. Not that that was a certain guide to character. After all, much against her will and now that he had dropped his curt suspicious manner, *she* found him charming and decidedly attractive. Why couldn't he have been old, bald, paunchy and sinister as she'd imagined him? she wondered a little irritably. It would have made her task a lot easier. As it was, she felt disturbed by her reactions to him. She actually felt guilty about the way she was deceiving him, using his hospitality and apparent good nature for her own ends.

She didn't take him up on his invitation to explore the house. She would eventually of course. Somewhere here might lie the clue to his interest in Anthony. But she was achingly tired. It was more than twenty-four hours since she'd had any solid sleep. She kicked off her shoes and lay down on the bed, intending only to relax for half an hour. Instead she fell into a profound slumber, and her watch showed half past six when she awoke.

Hastily Giana showered, renewed her make-up and scrambled into the only dress she had with her, of soft turquoise-coloured wool which turned her hazel eyes to greeny-blue. The long cheval mirror told her that she looked considerably better than when she'd arrived. The softly clinging dress emphasised her slender shapeliness, her long, lovely legs, the burgeoning fullness of surprisingly generous breasts. Then, as she realised she was appraising herself as if Breid Winterton's opinion of her appearance mattered, she swung away from the mirror and hurried downstairs.

Breid's assessment of her seemed cursory enough, yet Giana had the notion those cool grey eyes missed no detail of her appearance. She was a little piqued by his lack of comment, his closed expression. Yet she did not think it stemmed from discourtesy. He didn't strike her as being a discourteous man.

Their walk down to the village was a quiet one, but Giana felt the silence, broken only by the sound of the steady rain, was full of incomprehensible vibrations.

On closer inspection, the Cock and Bull turned out to be a very small hostelry indeed. It boasted only two guest rooms, Giana discovered, both of which were in use, so she wouldn't have been able to put up there. There was no dining-room as such, but they did do excellent bar food. She was surprised it was worth their while and said so.

'Oh, we get quite a lot of tourists,' Breid said. 'You'd be surprised. This part of Kent has quite a lot to offer in terms of historic buildings, churches, etc. It's not too bad at this time of year, but in summer the country lanes are crawling with cars. I find it a damned nuisance but it's good trade for the publicans.'

A fair number of Dinas Mead's residents drifted in and out of the bar while Giana and Breid were eating. Everyone seemed to know him, but it was obvious, too, that the acquaintance did not include familiarity. Their glances at Breid Winterton's tall, strikingly lovely companion were frankly curious, but their greetings to Breid himself were tinged with a respectful awe that puzzled

Giana. It seemed to accord him celebrity status. Granted he was a writer, but she had never heard of him. Giana smiled at everyone impartially, her full mouth with its long upper lip widening in a smile as generous as her compassionate nature. But Breid's reaction to their salutations was polite, nothing more.

She studied him covertly, wondering what thoughts and secrets lay behind that inscrutable face. He had a firm mouth with a full lower lip that ought to have held a hint of passion, but its lines were cold and his handsome features never seemed to be animated by a smile. In repose his expression was bleak and shuttered.

'What kind of writing do you do?' she ventured to ask him.

'Books,' he said almost off-handedly. 'I'll lend you one. You won't like it, but you may as well see the sort of stuff you'll be asked to type.'

'Why won't I like it?' she asked curiously. It seemed an odd thing for a writer to say and it didn't sound as if the remark were made from modesty.

'Perhaps because I write about life as I see it and I haven't found all that much in my life to rejoice about.'

Giana remembered the postmistress's hints about a tragedy in this man's past. She waited expectantly but nothing more was forthcoming. He was not, apparently, the kind of man who unburdened himself of his sorrows by sharing them with others. He might, perhaps, open up to his intimates, whoever they were. Giana wondered if there was a woman in Breid Winterton's life. He was attractive enough to have them flocking around him in swarms.

If he was reserved in talking about himself, neither did he ask her any questions, despite his forecast that they would get to know each other better. Giana was surprised to feel pique at his obvious lack of interest. She ought to have been relieved not to have to withstand his cross-questioning, but most of the men she encountered, either socially or through her work, seemed only too eager to learn more about her, whether their interest was merely friendly or would-be-flirtatious. She couldn't imagine Breid Winterton flirting.

'Shall we have coffee here or back at the house?' His deep voice startled her out of her reflective mood.

'Just as you like.'

'In that case we'll have it at home. It always tastes better somehow.' He paid their bill and waited impersonally for her to precede him through the low doorway. Giana, who was used to such courtesies, noted that there was no attempt on his part at guiding her, no hand hovered at her elbow. It shouldn't have been disconcerting, but it was.

Breid had facilities for making coffee in his office, she discovered.

'So I don't mess up the kitchen,' he explained quite seriously. It seemed that either Breid Winterton was very much in awe of his Mrs Pimblett—which seemed unlikely—or that he was a very considerate employer.

'I didn't ask you where you live,' he said after they had sipped in silence for a while. Again Giana had the impression that he was not talkative by inclination but felt obliged to make conversation of some kind.

'London.'

'Oh.' His eyebrows expressed surprise. 'What part?'

'Oh, SW1,' she said evasively. 'You probably wouldn't know the area.'

'Just a bedsit, I suppose,' he assumed. Then, sympathetically, 'Pretty dreary, aren't they, when you're out of work? I had some of that in my youth.'

In his youth. The expression made Giana look at him speculatively. She hadn't wondered about his age before. He read her questioning gaze and smiled briefly, as though it were an unaccustomed exercise.

'I'm thirty-nine. And you?'

'Twenty-four.'

'Good God. Almost young enough to be my daughter.' A sudden spasm of pain creased his face, but it was gone so suddenly Giana wondered if she'd imagined it.

'You'd have been a very young father.' But her attempt at a joke fell flat. He seemed to have switched off and gone somewhere she could not follow. His blue-grey eyes had darkened with the remoteness which sorrow or pain could leave; Giana had seen a lot of both in the course of her work.

At a loss for what to say or do, she averted her eyes and let her gaze roam around the study. It alighted upon the bookshelves.

'May I have a look at your books?' she asked.

'Yes, help yourself.' His voice was toneless and she jumped up, turning her back on him, more disturbed than she could have thought possible by the evidence of his unhappiness. She ought not to care how Breid Winterton felt.

'Goodness,' Giana discovered an instant later, 'they're all by one person. Oh, how stupid of me. They must be yours. But that means...' She turned back towards him, her pale, flawless complexion flushed with excitement. '*You're* Ruthven Murgatroyd?'

He didn't seem moved or flattered by her awe.

'That's my pen-name, yes.'

'My father simply loves your books. When he's finished one he can hardly wait for the next one to come out.'

She was relieved to see that some life had returned to the dark eyes and his face was less strained.

'And do you share your father's tastes?' He sounded faintly amused, though nothing of it showed in his features.

'I'm ashamed to confess I haven't read any of them.'

'Why be ashamed?' he demanded. 'They're certainly not everybody's cup of tea. In fact, I told you they probably wouldn't be to your taste.'

'Because my father says they're "literature" and I have a great respect for my father's opinion.'

'And why should you be ashamed of not reading "literature", as your father's kind enough to call it? I don't say I agree with him, mind.'

'Perhaps ashamed is the wrong word,' she admitted. 'But I don't quite know what else to call it. I'm a self-admitted low-brow. I can't help it; it's just the way I'm made. I don't like pop music, but I do prefer musical comedy to opera.'

'There's nothing wrong with that,' Breid told her. 'Actually, I like both.'

'And I read light, fast-moving books instead of great heavy dissertations.' She grimaced wryly. 'I once tried to read Dostoevsky. But no matter how hard I try, I prefer thick family sagas and witty Regency romances.'

'And I'll be bound you like television soap operas?' He was teasing her now and for the first time she saw him really smile. The effect was riveting and she had to swallow before she could answer him.

'Certainly not,' she said with dignity. 'They're rubbish. Nothing like real life. These scriptwriters should meet some of the people I...' She bit off what she'd been about to say and went on hastily, 'But I do watch a lot of TV, though only for entertainment. I'm not a great lover of documentaries or discussion programmes.'

'Again, what's wrong with that?' Breid asked. He seemed really interested now, his eyes intent on her lovely face. She was flushed now, animated by the strength of her self-defence.

'That's what I keep asking myself. Why should something obscure or difficult always be assumed to be best? If beauty is in the eye of the beholder, then interest should be in the mind of the reader or listener—or watcher, in the case of TV. But if you tell people that, they look at you as if you're inferior,' she concluded indignantly.

'Am *I* looking at you as if you're inferior?'

No, he wasn't. She wasn't quite sure what his intent gaze portended, but it made her uncomfortable again. She dragged her eyes away from his and looked at her watch.

'Goodness,' she said with false surprise. 'Is that really the time? If I'm going to start work for you tomorrow I'd better get some rest. Besides,' she rattled on, suddenly unaccountably nervous, 'I'm keeping you up with my silly chatter.'

'Not at all. I'm a night owl.' His manner was suddenly cynically weary again. 'There's not much point in going to bed when I don't sleep. I quite often work until two or three in the morning.'

'So then you have a lie-in?'

'Lord, no. I get up about seven and have a working breakfast. I'll probably want to start dictating about nine o'clock. Will that suit you?'

'Yes, of course.'

'I'll say goodnight then.' He rose politely but his glance towards his desk made her realise she'd been keeping him from his work which, by all accounts, was his main panacea against whatever it was that troubled him so deeply.

'Goodnight.' Now that the moment had come to leave him she felt oddly reluctant to go. That part of her nature which went out so freely to people in trouble or distress had been aroused. She found herself wanting him to confide in her, wishing there was something she could say or do to lift the heavy cloud from him.

This was ridiculous. She wasn't here to help Breid Winterton. For the last half-hour, she realised, she hadn't even given a single thought to Anthony or to the reason for her presence at Dinas Mead.

'Goodnight,' she said again.

Giana was still thinking about Breid Winterton as she climbed the wide, shallow steps of the oak staircase. They creaked gently beneath her feet. She liked what she'd seen so far of this gracious old manor house. And—she was dismayed to have to admit it—so far she rather liked Breid Winterton. How on earth, she puzzled, had Anthony got on the wrong side of a man like this?

She closed the bedroom curtains, switched on the colour-matched bedside lamp and undressed quickly in its light that bathed her body with a warm apricot glow. Unobtrusive background heating warmed the room, and her nightdress with thin shoulder-straps did not need the addition of its matching jacket.

She sat down at the dressing-table and began to brush her long, silky hair until it hung in a silvery veil about her bare shoulders. Mesmerised by the soothing rhythm of the hairbrush, she gazed into her mirrored eyes as though her image were a stranger whose thoughts she sought to read. Apart from the fact that he was having Anthony followed, Breid Winterton intrigued her. It wasn't just his looks, though she had to admit they'd exerted a powerful influence on her so that she couldn't believe him capable of any real wrong. There was a certain glamour, too, about his profession. But that didn't entirely account for the fascination she felt. It must be the air of tragedy he emanated that really pulled most strongly at her senses and aroused her curiosity.

Lost in her thoughts, Giana did not hear the knock which preceded the door's opening. Startled, she swung round on the dressing-table stool to see Breid Winterton's tall figure in the doorway. He was stooped slightly so that his head cleared the low frame.

'Oh!' In an instinctive gesture she folded her arms across the transparent material that draped her breasts. Her eyes wide, she stared at him, made nervous by this unlooked for intrusion.

'I'm sorry!' Incredibly, it was he who had coloured, or perhaps it was just the lamp-glow. 'I did knock. You forgot your handbag.' He came a little further into the room. 'And you did say you wanted to borrow a book. May I recommend you start with this one? It's not my first, but I think perhaps it's my best.'

She held out a hand which a fine tremor unsteadied.

'Thank you.' It came out as a whisper and she cleared her throat, repeated the words. 'Thank you.'

The book was in her hand, but Breid did not release it immediately, and Giana found herself unable to look away from that intent blue-grey gaze.

Then it was as if he deliberately snapped the thread of tension that seemed to stretch between them. He pushed the book at her in a gesture that was like a re-jection. And his 'goodnight' sounded almost angry.

Giana had thought she was tired, but Breid's visit had left her strangely restless and unsettled. Perhaps the book would help. She slid between the bedcovers, adjusted the bedside lamp and turned to the title page: *Don't Ask Why, Ask What For*, by Ruthven Murgatroyd. The quo-tation, she saw, was attributable to Carl Jung. Giana wasn't familiar with it. But then, she grimaced wryly, she wouldn't be. Low-brow, she muttered to herself. However, she was curious to see how Breid Winterton interpreted Jung's words.

The jacket blurb described the story as an in-depth study of a man's anger and despair, his questioning of life. It sounded rather daunting and Giana fully expected it to be difficult to read; that was her general experience of so-called 'literature'. But she was pleasantly sur-prised, hooked from the very first paragraph.

This was a love story, she discovered breathlessly, a sad one but a thrilling, gripping portrait of an emotion that endured even beyond death.

In the past Giana had found that male writers dealt quite differently with romantic love, that they tended towards over-sentimentality or sheer eroticism. Normally, when she was looking for real feeling she went to female writers. But here was a greater depth of emotion than she had ever encountered—between the covers of a book or in real life. Surely only a special kind of man could write this way?

She turned to the back cover. Thoughtfully she studied the photograph of the author. But the pictured likeness was as enigmatic as the man himself.

Giana was awake very early next morning. It had stopped raining. The central heating hadn't come on yet, and through the window she'd opened last night came a cool fresh smell that wasn't the dead dusty aroma of London. She was suddenly eager to be up. At heart she wasn't a city dweller. Until her marriage she had always lived in a small village and commuted to the nearest town each day, but since her marriage she had missed the countryside.

She pulled on an emerald-green tracksuit and a matching woolly hat and ran lightly downstairs. The front door was already unbolted and she stepped out into the damp chill of the garden. Her exploration took her round the side of the house, past the conservatory, down the long garden and through the shrubbery to the beechwood beyond. Last year's dead damp leaves muffled her footsteps as she walked beneath the tall, still dripping trees. It was a cheerless enough place on this morning in March, but Giana could imagine it in spring and summer. She wondered if Breid Winterton realised how privileged he was to have his own private woodland.

As she emerged on the far side she saw the man himself. He was in profile to her. He stood motionless, one foot resting on a fallen tree-trunk. His arms were folded and his gaze was fixed on the distant horizon of three oast cones and a stretch of tortuous ploughland. He was so still, so remote, that she feared to intrude on his privacy and turned back the way she'd come. But she must have made some sound, however slight, for he was aware of her presence.

'Good morning. I didn't expect you to be up so early. I'm afraid breakfast won't be ready for another hour yet.'

Giana waited for him to come up to her and they fell into step, back towards the house.

'Did you sleep well?' he asked.

'Yes, thank you.' She had to tilt her head to smile up at him. 'Once I'd managed to put your book down!'

'That sounds as though you found it tolerable?' he said quizzically.

'More than that!' she exclaimed warmly. Her hazel eyes were almost green with intensity. 'Oh, I wish I could think of the right words to express what I feel about it. It's so convincing, so sad and yet so beautiful. I almost forgot it was fiction.'

'Perhaps,' he said drily, 'that's because it isn't fiction. At least not entirely.'

'You mean all that really happened? To people you knew?'

'Yes.' It was said curtly. Clearly he didn't mean to expand on the subject.

'Well, even so, you had to put it into words and you have done, splendidly. I can't wait to read some more.'

It was impossible to tell whether or not her eulogy pleased him.

'You'll be seeing the new one through from start to finish,' he observed. 'That's if your enthusiasm doesn't wane after a few weeks of country life.'

'I love the country,' she told him with simple truth. It wouldn't be distaste for this beautiful spot that ended her association with him. She was disturbed to find that even the idea of not seeing Breid Winterton or Dinas Mead again made her feel strangely sad.

They breakfasted together and Breid introduced her to his housekeeper. Mary Pimblett was a motherly bustling body, the soul of efficient domesticity. Just as obviously, she was fond of her employer. Graciously, she accepted Giana's offer to carry the dirty dishes through to the kitchen but made it even clearer than Breid Winterton had done that this was her undisputed territory.

'Two women using the same kitchen always makes for trouble,' she said when Giana asked if she needed any further help. 'And so I told poor dear Mrs Winterton, God rest her soul. "Mary," she says, "you can have your kitchen with pleasure. I'd rather get on with my painting any day than wash pots".'

'Mrs Winterton?' Giana asked. 'Mr Winterton's mother?'

'Lord bless you, no. Didn't she die when Mr Breid and his sister was little more than babbies? And me brought in as a young woman to be their nursemaid, bless them. I'm talking about his wife.' Again she crossed herself. 'I hope, Miss Spencer,' she said with some severity, 'that you're going to last longer than his last two or three secretaries.' Giana hoped her guilt didn't show. 'Like a bear with a sore head he is when he can't get on with his writing. And who can blame him? It's the only thing that seems to take the poor lamb out of himself. And him such a good, fine man!'

'Poor lamb' seemed a very strange description to apply to the man who, for some reason, was having Anthony Leyburn's movements dogged. And yet Mrs Pimblett's words had been oddly moving—and convincing. Thoughtfully, Giana made her way from the kitchen to the study. Breid looked up from his desk.

'I'll be with you in a minute. I'm just looking through today's mail. Perhaps you'd like to be familiarising yourself with the word processor. The handbook's beside it. I'm told it's comparatively simple to operate.'

'Don't you use it then?'

'I know how to, but I can't abide mechanical devices. They come between me and the creative process. I dictate or write by... Blast and damnation!' So violent was the exclamation that Giana swung round to look at him. In one hand he held a long buff envelope from which he'd extracted a single sheet of paper.

'Not bad news I hope?' Giana ventured to ask.

'Certainly the worst I could hope to hear at this moment,' he said savagely. With an angry gesture he jerked open a drawer, thrust the offending missive inside and slammed the drawer shut. 'Right,' his tone was still grim, 'let's get on with some work.' He began to pace the room, speaking rapidly.

As her hand raced over the pages of her shorthand notebook, Giana wondered if he always thought this fast or whether his still simmering fury had accelerated his pace. At first, panic-stricken, she wondered if she would be able to keep up with him; it was quite a while since she'd done any sustained note-taking. She was scribbling outlines according to sound only, the meaning lost to her.

But as the work progressed Breid slowed to a more moderate rate. With increasing confidence Giana found herself able to understand what she was writing. She was disappointed to find that this was no love story. It was about violent death, the law, about trial, justice, revenge. In a way it reminded her of Anthony's articles. It was to be a different kind of book altogether and yet it was by the same author and had the same sense of despair and loss as the other. Nevertheless it was still a compelling narrative. Giana was no fool and she was beginning to suspect that the source of Breid's material lay closer to home than someone he merely knew, that in fact it came from within himself.

She realised he had stopped dictating and turned to look questioningly at him, only to find him standing close to her chair, his eyes fixed attentively upon her. She swallowed. For the second time in their acquaintance she was aware of something tenuous but vibrant stretching between them as their gazes locked.

'Is...is anything wrong?' she asked.

'No!' he said abruptly. Then, 'It's just that at certain angles you remind me of…of someone.' He moved away and whatever it was that linked them snapped.

Apparently his creative mood was broken, too.

'Start transcribing that lot, will you? I need some fresh air.' He left the room via the conservatory.

It only took a few minutes with the handbook for Giana to reacquaint herself with the workings of the word processor. She had almost finished her transcription, finding the story even more absorbing now she had leisure to appreciate it, when a particularly arresting thought occurred to her. She was behaving as if her sole purpose for being at Dinas Mead was to further Breid Winterton's writing career, whereas she should be taking every opportunity to acquaint herself with his private affairs, and where better to start than with his mail?

With a nervous glance towards the conservatory door she moved towards Breid's desk. He had tidily discarded the envelopes and the letters were neatly stacked in his in-tray. Her fingers trembled as she rifled through them. A publisher's contract, forwarded fan-mail, a stationer's bill. Nothing incriminating there. Then she remembered the letter he'd thrust out of sight.

It was all too easy. The drawer wasn't locked. It slid smoothly open and Giana found herself staring at a thick sheet of paper embossed with a familiar name—Ellis and Palmer.

She bent closer to read the short message. It told Breid Winterton that Anthony Leyburn had somehow evaded Mr Ellis's vigilance and left London about two weeks ago, in the last week of February, and that he had, to all intents and purposes 'vanished into thin air'. 'Do you wish me,' the letter concluded, 'to pursue my investigations?' Though Giana had been hoping to find something about Breid Winterton's connection with Anthony, she hadn't expected anything like this. She read the letter again, and forgot as she did so to be vigilant.

'What the hell do you suppose you're doing?'

Giana looked up so quickly that she ricked her neck. But the pain was as nothing beside her apprehension as she stared across the desk into Breid Winterton's handsome, angry face.

CHAPTER THREE

'SNOOPING, Giana?' His cold gaze was more grey than blue now.

In the split second between discovery and defence Giana had decided the only way was to brazen it out. She could hardly deny she'd been reading Breid's private correspondence.

'Yes,' she said with a defiant tilt of her head, and saw his thick dark eyebrows, such a contrast to the silvered fair hair, start up into his hairline. He hadn't expected that. 'I wanted to know what had annoyed you so much. After all,' she went on quickly before he could say anything, 'if I'm going to be your secretary...' It was a lame excuse and her voice faltered away as he moved towards her.

He came round the desk and stood beside her. A strong hand on her shoulder turned her towards him. Apprehensively she looked up into his face. It was hard to fathom his expression but his mouth was a straight hard line. His free hand grasped her chin.

'Can you look me in the eyes and tell me that's all it was?' Fortunately for Giana he didn't wait for an answer. 'Why should I believe you?' And this she could answer.

'No reason, I suppose,' she admitted. Her shoulders slumped. 'You'll want me to leave, of course.' She felt decidedly depressed. It was because she'd failed so early in her mission, she told herself.

'No,' he surprised her by saying. 'If you're telling the truth, why should I get rid of you?' With difficulty Giana repressed a shudder as, with grim emphasis, he went on, 'And if you do have some ulterior motive I'd rather have you where I can keep my eye on you. But I'll tell you this, if it were not for that glowing recommendation from your previous employers... Just remember one thing, Giana, you're here to help me with my work. My private affairs are none of your concern. Understood?'

She nodded dumbly, and was relieved when he released her. His grasp had been hard and compelling and, though he'd caught her prying, her reaction to his closeness had been unwilling fascination rather than fear. Whatever else he might be, Breid Winterton was a magnetically attractive man. For those few moments she'd been very aware of him, disturbingly so, and that was a complication she didn't need.

Ellis and Palmer's letter was certainly food for thought. Giana pondered on it as she completed her transcription. It made it seem there might be more to Anthony's prolonged absence than a secret, extended assignment. Giana found her reactions strangely mixed. Concern for Anthony's safety mingled with regret at Breid's apparent involvement in her husband's disappearance. She *liked* Breid Winterton.

Breid suggested an early lunch break; he always lunched at the Cock and Bull, he told her. They set off, Giana well wrapped up against the cold March wind. Clad only in slacks and a chunky white pullover, Breid seemed impervious to the weather.

'The walk there and back gives me a break from my work,' he explained. 'That's the only snag about writing. You live "over the shop", so to speak.'

The rain was still holding off and a watery sun held a faint promise of warmer days ahead. Giana suspected that Breid would prefer to walk in the brooding silence which seemed habitual with him, but she would learn nothing from his silences.

'Have you always been a writer?' She ventured the non-controversial question.

'In one way or another.' At first she thought this was to be her only answer but another stride or two and he went on. 'I conceived the idea while I was still up at Oxford that as well as reading books I would enjoy writing them. Obviously it wasn't practical to become "a writer" *per se*; I had to earn a living. So in the first instance I went in for journalism.'

'How long ago was that?' Breid was a slighter older man; Anthony was thirty-five. But they might have been colleagues at some stage in their careers.

'I gave it up about three years ago when I discovered in myself a distaste for journalism and journalists.'

'Oh! Why?'

'Why do you want to know?' he asked abruptly. 'What possible interest can my career or my likes and dislikes hold for you?'

'I'm interested in people,' Giana said truthfully. It was one of the reasons she'd become a nurse. That and her urge to relieve suffering. Without conceit, she added, 'And I've been told I'm a good listener.'

Breid allowed her to precede him through the open door of the Cock and Bull. Again she noticed that, unlike

most men, he made no attempt to place a guiding hand
at her elbow.

'And I suppose you find most people respond to that
wide-eyed, ingenuous stare of yours?' There was faint
amusement in the blue-grey eyes. 'I'll remember that—
in the unlikely event of my ever needing a confidante.'
Then, on a note of suspicion, 'Are you sure you haven't
some deeper reason for quizzing me than an interest in
human nature?'

Giana hoped the redness of her cheeks would be at-
tributed to their walk in the biting wind.

'What other reason could I have?' she fenced.

'I don't know.' He regarded her consideringly as he
handed her the bar menu and then there was silence while
they studied it. He placed their order and suggested they
take advantage of being the first there to occupy the
inglenook seat, close to the cheerful log fire. He seemed
to have forgotten or perhaps deliberately abandoned their
earlier topic.

Giana reopened it.

'Surely you can't dislike *all* journalists. You can't
generalise like that. They can't all be bad.'

'Perhaps not,' he admitted. 'I flatter myself I for one
didn't stoop to some of the methods employed by the
Press. But,' he added, 'it becomes rather different when
you're on the receiving end of their attentions. There's
one Johnny in particular...' He stopped as the publi-
can's wife brought their ploughman's lunches and two
halves of bitter shandy, and Giana waited breathlessly
for him to continue. '...he's a reporter with one of those
scurrilous sensation-seeking rags. He enjoys a repu-

tation for being as unprincipled as his employers. He'll stop at nothing to get "copy".'

Giana had no doubt that he was talking about Anthony.

'And you've had personal experience of his methods?'

'I have. Not once but twice. And now... But that's another story. Suppose you fill me in on your background? Where do you hail from—originally I mean? You don't sound to me like a Londoner born and bred?'

'I'm not. I was born in Hertfordshire, in a village not far from Bishop's Stortford. I don't suppose you've ever heard of Stortford? It's main claim to fame is that it was the birthplace of Cecil Rhodes.'

'I've heard of it. One result of a journalistic career is a fair knowledge of geography.'

'My father's a vicar, my mother helps with the parish work. And that's about it—my life story I mean.'

'Any brothers or sisters?'

'No.'

'Is there a boyfriend left behind in London?'

She was able to shake her head. She hadn't left anyone behind in the sense he meant. Since his manner was more relaxed, she dared to tease.

'I can well believe you were once a journalist. You're beginning to sound like one.' Immediately she regretted her remark. His face closed up.

'I beg your pardon. I was merely making conversation, since you seem to be disposed to do so.' He stood up, his head bent to avoid the low-beamed ceiling. 'I'll get our bill. Unless you want another drink?' It sounded like a polite formality.

'No, thanks,' she said hastily, then, with an attempt at lightening the atmosphere, 'I'm not used to it. I'll be falling asleep over my desk.' She wondered what he would look like if he smiled—really smiled—not this cold, polite grimace that passed as a response to her remark.

'I think I can guarantee to keep you awake.' His tone became grim. 'The contents of my next chapter can hardly be called bedtime reading.'

None of his books could be called that, Giana thought that night, as she avidly devoured the rest of the one she'd borrowed. But they were interesting. And he would be an interesting man to work for. She found herself almost regretting that their association would be so short.

Breid was certainly a hard taskmaster. His hours of work were as irregular and demanding as he had promised. He seemed a different man, less aloof, when he was working. During dictation he would pause sometimes to consult a reference work. Occasionally Giana had to help him search through his deplorably untidy filing system for an elusive piece of information. At times like this he talked more easily and, though most of their conversations were confined to work, a certain mental rapport built up between them. Giana found herself liking him more and more.

Over meals their topics were more generalised and they found many likes and dislikes in common. But she learned most about the private Breid Winterton from his books. If she had needed any confirmation, she learned that he was certainly not a happy man. On nearly every page his private anguish showed through the writing. But Giana had no doubt, as Mrs Pimblett had said, that Breid was a good man, that he deplored the crime and violence he so vividly portrayed. She could see why her father, a man of immense rectitude, admired his work.

One thing puzzled her: none of his books seemed to have a 'happy ending'. True, criminals were brought to justice, but the main protagonists, the victims of crime, were left in their unhappiness, with no gleam of hope for the future that Giana could detect. Surely most readers preferred a satisfactory denouement. She could only suppose that Breid's popularity with his editors and his readers alike lay in the power and beauty of his prose, the gripping nature of his subject matter.

Giana had been at Dinas Mead about ten days when Breid announced that he had to go up to London for a few days. She half hoped he might ask her to accompany him, but he didn't suggest it; quite the reverse.

'I'm not sure how long I'll be away, but I think I've left you enough work. If not,' drily, 'the filing cabinets could do with a little reorganisation.'

Giana worked hard while Breid was away, but she also took the opportunity to do something else he'd suggested. She explored the house, choosing the housekeeper's afternoon off to do so. She felt sure Mrs Pimblett wouldn't approve of such curiosity, whatever her employer might have said.

Though large, the old manor was surprisingly compact. The ground floor held no surprises. Not even a systematic search of Breid's desk revealed his interest in Anthony Leyburn. The attics were surprisingly clutter-free, as were the spare rooms, and that left only Breid's bedroom.

Giana felt a strong distaste for what she must do. She had to summon up all her resolution, remind herself of her reasons for being at Dinas Mead before she could bring herself to cross the threshold of the master bedroom. She left the door wide open in case Mrs Pimblett returned early and she had to beat a swift retreat.

Breid's room was the largest on the upper floor and almost spartan in its contents. The colour scheme was in very masculine browns and creams. There was no indication that any woman had ever shared the vast double bed with him. Giana would have expected a man of such strong sentiment to have retained mementoes of his wife's occupancy.

An enormous wardrobe—modern fitted ones would have been incongruous in this house—held a modest though well-cut assortment of clothes. A swift search of pockets elicited nothing but a subtle male fragrance that brought Breid into the room as surely as his physical presence would have done; and Giana's sense of guilt mounted. A tallboy held folded shirts and underwear and Giana felt her face glow with embarrassed heat as she slid her hands beneath the neat piles of more intimate garments, searching for she knew not what.

Nothing. With a sigh that was almost one of relief Giana turned to leave the room, then stopped short, a strangled gasp rising in her throat.

For a moment she thought she'd been caught red-handed. But the eyes that met hers belonged to no living creature.

On the wall opposite the bed, where it must be the last thing Breid saw at night and the first thing each morning, hung a full length portrait. Until this moment the open door had concealed it from Giana's gaze.

With a growing sense of perplexity she studied the painting. It portrayed a tall, slender woman. She was blonde, strikingly good-looking with the merriest eyes imaginable and a large generous mouth endowed with a long upper lip. Giana had the oddest feeling that she was confronted by an old acquaintance. She moved closer.

In the bottom right hand corner, in tiny lettering so unobtrusive as to be almost invisible, she read, 'portrait of the artist' and the signature, 'Francesca Winterton'.

So this was Breid's late wife. And as Giana continued her study of the painted face the sense of recognition grew upon her, became certainty. This was how *she* might look in another ten years' time. She, Giana, could have passed for Francesca Winterton's younger sister.

It was impossible for Breid not to have noticed the resemblance. She remembered his startled double-take the first time he'd seen her. She recalled the remark he'd made—that she reminded him of someone. But in that case her presence in his house could only be a constant needlessly painful reminder of his loss. She was surprised that he'd let her stay.

'Snooping *again*, Giana?'

The expression 'I nearly leapt a foot in the air' came into Giana's mind. It had always seemed a foolish one. Now she knew it wasn't the physical self that took that terrifying jump but the heart. For an instant hers had seemed to leave her body, then plunge with a sickening jerk.

Unseen, unheard, Breid Winterton had returned and now his tall figure filled the doorway, standing between her and escape. His attractive features, which until now she had mostly seen set in lines of quiet pain, were animated by a mixture of emotions she could not fathom. Certainly there was anger there. And he had every right to be angry. But there was something more, something nameless, which disturbed her even more.

'I ... You did say I could explore the house.'

'But why this room? What possible interest could my bedroom hold for you?' He didn't give her time to answer but advanced upon her. The glint in his grey eyes boded no good.

As, instinctively, she backed away, his hands shot out and gripped her shoulders. The check to her impetus made her stumble on the thick carpet and she fell clumsily against him. For an instant, her body pressed closely to his, they swayed together and she heard his sharp intake of breath before, almost roughly, he restored her balance. His hands had fallen to his side as though he regretted his impulse to grab her.

'Why this room?' he repeated. 'And what interest does that portrait hold for you?'

'None. I mean I didn't know the portrait was there until I turned round to leave the room.'

'Which you did as soon as you realised it was my room and that you had no business here?' It was said sarcastically, sceptically. His keen gaze scanned the room. And, remembering her thorough search through his most intimate possessions, Giana flushed scarlet. She felt an almost irresistible urge to look behind her to reassure herself that she had closed the wardrobe doors and drawers, to see whether she'd left any trace of her activities. But such a glance would betray her.

'I would have left immediately if I hadn't seen the portrait.' A vivid picture of her father's disapproving face flashed across her inward vision, and she imagined his censure could he know of the lies she had told directly or indirectly since she'd been at Foxdene Manor. 'It was necessary, Dad,' she could imagine herself pleading.

'You've never seen this portrait before—reproduced in newspapers or magazines?'

'Never!' She didn't understand the intensity behind the question but thank God she could answer truthfully. The relief she felt gave an added vehemence to her denial, to the clarity of her hazel gaze, and she saw Breid relax, knew he believed her.

'But now you've seen it, you must have realised something?' He watched her intently.

'I...I'm a little like her,' she said hesitantly, afraid of giving offence, of presuming where the woman he'd loved was concerned.

'A *little* like her!' It was a growl of pain. 'My God! You're damnably like her—or as she was twenty years ago, when we were first married.'

There was so much anguish in his face that Giana could hardly bear to look at him. She wanted to run from him, to leave him to recover, but he still blocked her way. Equally her warm, compassionate heart made her want to reach out to him, as she wished it were in her power to comfort him.

'I'm sorry,' was all she could say. In the face of this man's grief, the practised ease with which she attempted to console her patients or bereaved relatives had utterly deserted her. Just the thought of extending a friendly hand, or, as she had done in some cases, offering an embrace, a shoulder to cry on, stirred her unbearably in a way she had never felt stirred before. It was almost a sexual longing, she discovered uneasily. 'Perhaps you'd rather I didn't go on working for you? It must be painful...' She tried to edge a way past him.

'No. Wait.' He made no move. Just his tone was enough to detain her. 'Francesca's been dead a long time. Over the years I've learnt to live with it. Most of the time it's just a dull knowledge of a loss that can never be replaced. Just occasionally it hits me hard. Like the moment you walked into my life and for a second I thought... In a way having you here is almost like having her back.' He gave a grating laugh. 'It sounds ridiculous, doesn't it, at my age, playing games of pretend? But sometimes I've tried to imagine you *are* Francesca.' And, as Giana shifted uneasily, 'Oh, don't worry...' His voice was harshly mocking, but whether of her or of himself Giana couldn't decide. 'That's as far as it goes. I'm not asking you to stand in for her in any other sense of the word.'

Again that strange longing stirred within Giana and she wished he would let her pass. She didn't want to be involved in his private emotions. She didn't want to feel sorry for him or to feel this urgent need to help him. Her judgement of him had to remain cool, clear and analytical. She still felt certain that Anthony's mysterious disappearance had some connection with Breid Winterton's surveillance of his activities.

Several times while Breid had been away she had telephoned the flat at Godolphin Buildings but there had been no reply. Her belongings had been forwarded to the *poste restante* address she'd given Fay, together with a message. Neither Fay nor her husband had heard anything of Anthony's whereabouts.

'I said I doubted I'd need a confidante, didn't I?' Breid's tone of voice was still gratingly self-deprecating. He moved restlessly about the room, one hand ruffling his silver-streaked blond hair; Giana could have left now, but she didn't. 'Ironically,' he went on, and his tone was ironic, 'it seems I may have to call on your assistance after all. Better my secretary,' it was a bitter rider, 'an uninvolved stranger, than my sister or any of my friends.'

It shouldn't do, but somehow his casual dismissal of her connection with him hurt.

'Naturally if there's any way I can help,' she said stiffly.

'Any way, Giana? Without reservation?' He stopped his pacing and his blue-grey eyes scrutinised her reaction. She couldn't help the nervous start, her instinctive glance towards the door. But he had said he didn't want her as a wife-substitute, she reminded herself. 'Are you even prepared to help me in a way that may compromise your own integrity?'

'You mean,' she hazarded, 'in something that may be outside the law?'

'Exactly! And I must have your promise, Giana. You're either with me in this or against me. No half measures.'

Heavens! Giana was beginning to think she'd bitten off more than she could chew. And yet this sounded promising. It could be a lead to Anthony's whereabouts. She was aware that her husband often teetered dangerously close to law-breaking to obtain his stories. She took a deep breath.

'I promise.'

'So easily?' He sounded suspicious and his eyes were still intent. 'I expected doubts, questions, even an out-right refusal.'

'Oh, there'll be questions,' she assured him. 'I can't help you if I don't know what it's all about. But you wouldn't answer questions without my promise, would you?'

He shook his head but his expression remained thoughtful.

'But no doubts? You're not afraid of what you might be getting into?'

'Yes,' she answered him with the honesty she pre-ferred. 'But I've never allowed fear to stop me tackling a job that's put in front of me.' And for an instant she thought there was a spark of appreciation, of ad-miration even, in the usually cool grey eyes.

'Francesca had that sort of courage,' he began, then stopped on a pained intake of breath. It was as if the words had escaped him against his will. Then he went on resolutely. 'I'm sorry. It's a long time since I've talked to anyone about my wife—or about any member of my family. But if you're going to help me you're entitled to know some of the details.'

Giana waited expectantly throughout the ensuing long silence.

'Leyburn, Anthony Leyburn,' he said suddenly, so suddenly that she started, thinking it was an accusation. Wide-eyed she stared at Breid, relaxing only as he went on. 'The letter you saw in my desk. No doubt you've wondered why I was having Leyburn followed by a private enquiry agent?'

'Yes.'

'He's the journalist I mentioned.'

'I guessed he might be. The one whose methods you don't approve of?'

'Right! And at this moment I believe his methods include making unscrupulous use of my daughter. I suspect he's having an affair with her.'

That Anthony was having an affair came as no surprise. Giana had always known that he flattered women, flirted with them, 'used' them in so far as he 'charmed' information out of them. This was merely an extension of his activities. What was a shock was that the woman involved should be Breid's daughter. It also made certain things a little clearer.

'What makes you think he's having an affair with your daughter?' she made herself ask in deliberately steady tones.

'She's been seeing him regularly for the past six months,' Breid said.

'Mightn't there be some other explanation?'

'She's infatuated with him. Tina wouldn't believe me,' he went on, 'when I warned her he probably wasn't in love with her, that he was just using her to get a story of some kind. Even though I told her how he'd behaved on other occasions—on the occasion when my wife and child . . .'

As he stopped abruptly Giana looked questioningly at him.

'Yes,' his tone was bitter. 'Francesca and I would have had two daughters.'

'Would have had?' Giana enquired gently. 'I knew your wife was dead but . . .'

'Mary Pimblett I suppose?' And as she nodded, 'Mary has always considered herself *in loco parentis* to my sister Vicky and me. Mary would like to see me married again.' A visible shudder ran through him. 'As if I'd be fool enough to give any more hostages to fortune. Anyway,' impatiently, 'we're straying from the point. When I found Tina was still seeing Leyburn in spite of everything I'd told her, I decided to have him followed. I wanted to find out what story he's working on and where Tina comes into it. I've been making some enquiries while I was in London.' He paused, then, 'Tina disappeared on the same day that Leyburn left town.'

'How old is your daughter?' Unaware that she did so, Giana slipped into her professional manner.

'Nineteen.'

'What does she do? Her job, I mean?'

'Nothing. Nothing at all. Not just because I make her an allowance—which I do, of course. She's my daughter, dammit,' he said almost defensively, 'and I can't see her starve, can I?'

'Of course not,' Giana assured him sympathetically. 'How do you get on with her?'

He grimaced.

'Not very well! Oh, I dare say it's as much my fault as hers. Don't think I haven't done a lot of heart-searching, blamed myself. Tina lost her mother at a time when she probably needed guidance most and I shut myself away more and more with my writing. The only other person who might have helped, my sister, lives in the South of France. Tina's fond of Vicky. But Vicky has her own family to look after. Anyway, the upshot of it was Tina refused to stay on at school, then got in with a bad set, teenagers who believed the world owed them a living, so they weren't prepared to work for it.'

'Where does she live?' Just in time Giana prevented herself from asking if Tina Winterton lived in the house at Makepeace Gardens. She wasn't supposed to know Breid's London address. 'With you?' she substituted.

'No. She insisted on having her own flat. God knows what goes on there.' Bitterly, 'If you ever get married, Giana, don't have children. They only mean heartbreak. In fact, don't get married.' The withdrawn brooding look was back in his grey-blue eyes again and somehow Giana couldn't bear it. She sought to divert his thoughts.

'What kind of story could Ant . . . this journalist want from your daughter?'

'I can only think it's something to do with the drugs scene.'

'Tina takes drugs?' Poor man. No wonder he exuded such an air of tragedy. Bereaved of his wife and one child and his only remaining daughter going off the rails. Such tragedies knew no class distinctions or social barriers.

'Not as far as I know. I hope to God she doesn't. I'm sure some of her so-called friends do. But I think Leyburn might be after bigger game than Tina and her friends.'

'The men behind the drug trade?'

'Yes. And the fact that he's gone to ground makes me think he may be getting somewhere.'

'Couldn't that kind of investigation be dangerous?' Giana's voice shook slightly but Breid didn't seem to notice.

'You can say that again! If that's what he's up to he's playing with fire and he's dragging my daughter into danger, too, damn him.'

Giana was frankly appalled by Breid's theory and her feelings were decidedly mixed. Even though she knew her marriage had been a mistake, she wouldn't want to see her husband come to harm. Twelve months of marriage must count for something.

'I'm going back to London tomorrow,' Breid broke in on her thoughts, 'And I'd like you to come with me.'

'Of course.' If he was going to London that was exactly where she wanted to be if she were to find out what Anthony was up to. She had to know for certain. And what then? she asked herself. What if he *was* just having an affair and not working on a story at all? One step at a time, she told herself firmly. She'd cross that bridge when she came to it.

'Apart from anything else,' Breid said wryly, 'having you in London will enable me to keep eye on *you*.'

'Oh!' She flushed. Her first reaction was indignation. 'You still don't trust me, do you?' But it wasn't pleasant knowing that he had good grounds for distrusting her. 'What do you plan to do in London?' she added quickly.

'Something I couldn't let Ellis and Palmer do. If Tina is mixed up with drug-pushers and old Ellis found anything incriminating, he might feel bound to go to the police.'

'That's why you want me,' Giana said bitterly. 'You think I'd be less scrupulous?'

His quiet reply reproached her.

'I'm trying to keep my daughter out of trouble. And I want an unbiased witness.' His good-looking face

wrinkled with distaste. 'God knows I hate the necessity.
I deplore the invasion of anyone's privacy.' Again Giana
flushed consciously. 'But I'm going to search Tina's flat.
I must.'

'If Tina and Ant . . . and Leyburn are having an affair,
their disappearance might have nothing to do with a news
story. They could just have gone off somewhere
to . . . to . . .' She didn't know how to put it.

'True. And if that's all it is I suppose I'll just have to
accept the situation and hope that Leyburn will eventually show himself in his true colours. But if he *is* in-
volving Tina in something else, something dangerous . . .'
He had no need to complete his sentence. Looking at
his face, Giana thought she wouldn't like to be in
Anthony's shoes if and when Breid Winterton caught up
with him.

They left Dinas Mead just after lunch next day.

'We could take the opportunity to call in at your flat
and pick up some more of your belongings,' Breid suggested as they drove towards London. His car was an
old but immaculately maintained Rolls Royce.

'Oh, no!' Giana said hastily. And, as the look he
darted at her seemed to be a suspicious one, 'Fay—my
friend—sent me enough clothes, etc, for the time being.'

'Don't you want to see if the place is all right? It could
have been broken into or . . .'

'My friend's keeping an eye on it,' she assured him.

The only thing she really wanted to do while she was
in London was to look in on old Mrs Hibbs. The old
lady would be wondering why she hadn't called lately.
But Giana wasn't sure she'd get the opportunity and she

wouldn't be back in London permanently for another two weeks, the remainder of her leave. If she didn't discover something about Anthony within those remaining weeks... In helping Breid Winterton she could even be on the wrong track. Anthony's absence from town might have nothing to do with Tina Winterton's disappearance.

They went first to Makepeace Gardens. Breid telephoned Ellis and Palmer.

'No news,' he told Giana wearily. 'Want to freshen up before we go round to Tina's flat?'

'No, I'm all right. And you want to get this over, don't you?' she said shrewdly.

From Breid's description of his daughter and her friends, Giana had been expecting a rather squalid dwelling. But Tina Winterton's flat was in a respectable area. It was cluttered and untidy but the three rooms—bedroom-cum-sitting-room, kitchen and bathroom—were nicely furnished and clean.

'Good God!' Breid looked around the main living area in despair. 'Where to start? Women and their passion for possessions!'

'Not all women!' Giana felt moved to retort.

'Sorry, I suppose I was generalising again. Actually, despite the fact that she was an artist, Francesca was exceptionally tidy.' A spasm of pain crossed his face. Then he said with a sympathetic look at Giana, 'I suppose if you've been out of work you can't afford all this kind of stuff.' He gestured around him.

'I suggest we start in here,' she said hastily, unwilling to be drawn into a further web of deception. She hesitated. 'Do you want me to search, too? What are we looking for?'

'Damned if I know.'

'Drugs?' she suggested.

'I hope not. I was thinking more in terms of a diary? Letters? Anything that might give us a clue where she's gone and if she is with Leyburn.'

For an hour they searched diligently and Giana thought it was going to be hopeless. Whatever Breid Winterton might believe to the contrary, she, too, hated going through someone else's possessions.

It was in a kitchen drawer used as a makeshift file for bills, receipts and other household trivia that Breid found the little bundle of letters. With a lurch of her stomach Giana recognised Anthony's handwriting. They sat on opposite sides of the small kitchen table. Breid untied the string that bound the letters and thrust half of them towards her.

'Are you sure you want me to read these?' But at his impatient gesture she opened the first envelope.

They were love letters. There was no mistaking that. Giana had never received any letters from Anthony before their marriage; their courtship had been too brief and they'd seen each other every day. She felt her cheeks burning hotly as she read the passionate lines. Anthony had never used language like this to her, not even during their lovemaking. She felt doubly betrayed; for, despite her growing doubts, she'd never been unfaithful to him. A choked noise escaped her. To her horror she felt her eyes fill with tears. One escaped to trickle down her cheek.

'Giana?' It was too much to expect that Breid wouldn't have noticed her distress. 'What is it?' He leaned across the table and took the letter from her. Quickly he scanned its contents, then he gave her a puzzled look. 'What's upsetting you?'

She had a good answer ready, one that was in essence true. She rubbed the back of her hand across her eyes in an almost childish gesture that the man found curiously endearing.

'It will probably sound awfully stupid to you,' she muttered, 'but . . . but no one's ever said those kind of things to me.'

'Poor kid!' In an impulsive gesture he reached across the table and took hold of her hand. 'But you're still young,' he said encouragingly. 'Time enough to meet Mr Right, eh?'

'I suppose so.' She gave him a watery smile. His hand was warm and strong and infinitely comforting. Involuntarily her fingers curled about his and she felt him respond.

'That's better.' He seemed to realise then what he was doing. His hand was removed and he said brusquely, 'Let's get on. Or would you rather I read the rest?'

'No, I'm all right now, honestly. I'm not usually so stupid. I expect it's because I'm tired.'

'Would you rather we packed it in? Finished the rest tomorrow?' But she sensed he didn't really want to stop now.

'No, let's finish the job.'

They read on. Giana was learning a great deal about her husband that she hadn't known. And a great deal about their marriage, she thought wryly. It seemed she hadn't been the only one to feel dissatisfaction.

'Tina, I'm a different man when I'm with you,' Anthony had written. 'You make me feel like a man.

You need me. My wife's so damned self-sufficient. I suppose it's her work. She's used to being supportive and efficient. She doesn't need anyone to lean on.'

'Leyburn's married, of course!' Breid said suddenly.

'Oh?' Giana felt her breath catch in her throat.

'He mentions his wife. But not by name.' Giana let the breath out on a careful sigh of relief. 'She sounds a pretty hard-boiled sort. A nurse. Probably the stiff, starchy type and obviously not interested in her husband's problems. "Charity begins at home".'

'Sick people would be in a mess without nurses!' Giana couldn't hold back the indignant retort.

'I'm not denying it. But when a career drives a wedge between husband and wife...'

'How do you know it was that way? Did *your* wife's career affect your marriage?' a still annoyed Giana wanted to know, and she saw Breid's face darken. He pushed back his chair and stood up.

'Quite the reverse, actually, but we'll leave me and Francesca out of this if you don't mind. If Leyburn's marriage had been working out, maybe he wouldn't have needed to run around with Tina.' He returned to his perusal of the letters and, though she was still seething, Giana followed his example.

'These letters don't tell us a damned thing about where to start looking for them.' Breid was pacing the room now as he read, rustling impatiently through the closely written pages.

'You still mean to find her, then?' Giana asked. 'Even though it's not what you originally thought?'

'I still mean to find her,' he confirmed grimly.

'There's something here that might help,' Giana said after a while. 'In this letter he mentions something called "The Retreat". He makes it sound somewhere rather special.'

'What? Let me see!' He moved behind her and actually snatched the letter. In doing so his hand brushed accidentally against Giana's breast and she felt the strangest tremor of sensation run through her entire body.

'It sounds as if it might be a regular rendezvous,' she suggested somewhat unsteadily. How often, when Anthony had been 'on an assignment', had he been with Tina Winterton? But she knew it wasn't that thought which had quickened her breathing.

Breid had not noticed her agitation. He threw down the letters. His fists were clenched on the table top. His normally handsome features were drawn into pugnacious lines, the well-shaped mouth was hard with annoyance. No, more than annoyance. He was absolutely furious.

'How dare she take him *there*? How dare she!'

Giana shivered. She was glad he wasn't angry with her.

'You know the place?'

'Know it! Good God!' He stood up abruptly and turned away. One stride took him the width of the small kitchen and he stood, shoulders hunched, leaning on the stainless steel sink. He appeared to be looking out of the window but Giana had a notion he saw nothing of the city street outside. There was tension in every line of his tall, lean body.

She waited. She knew from experience that there was a time to nudge people into confiding and a time to wait until they themselves were ready to talk.

At last he drew in a long, deep breath, as though in a deliberate attempt at relaxation. But his voice was still taut.

'Come on! Let's get out of here.'

'You're sure we've found what you're looking for?'

'No, I'm not sure. But I've a damned good suspicion. In any event I've found out enough for one day.' His eyes were still shadowed, his features hard and cold. 'It means we'll be off again tomorrow, on what might be a wild-goose chase. Are you still with me in this, Giana?'

She sensed a certain urgency in the question and her hazel eyes met his steadily.

'Yes.'

Briefly his hand touched her arm.

'Thanks. I'd appreciate your company. I don't relish going to The Retreat on my own. In fact I swore I'd never set foot in the place again.'

CHAPTER FOUR

BREID must make a considerable amount of money from his writing, Giana thought later that evening, when she'd had time to take in more of her surroundings at Twenty-seven, Makepeace Gardens.

He had this town house and his country home. True, there was only a housekeeper at Dinas Mead, but in London he had a full complement of servants. Money might not be everything—it obviously hadn't made Breid a happier man—but it could certainly smooth your path through life and buy you its comforts. Although Breid and Giana had been very late returning to the town house, a substantial dinner had been elegantly served in the panelled dining-room, with no sign of panic or resentment on the part of Breid's staff. They were probably very well paid for their services but Giana sensed, too, the very real devotion to their employer evinced by everyone, from the staid housekeeper down to the maid.

Over dinner, in front of the hovering maidservant, who, fortunately, had not recognised Giana, Breid made no reference to their recent quest. But later, when coffee had been served in the graciously furnished drawing-room, he reopened the subject.

They were sitting facing each other on two comfortable leather chesterfields that stood at right angles to a classically pedimented fireplace.

'You really are prepared to continue on this wild-goose chase, Giana? You'd be entitled to refuse. It has nothing to do with the work I hired you for. Would you rather stay in London and rejoin me at Dinas Mead when I send for you? If you give me your home address...'

'Oh, no! That is...I'd rather come with you,' she said quickly. 'Unless you'd rather I didn't? It's up to you.'

'As I told you, I'd be glad of your company.' He sighed and his face clouded over. 'As you've probably gathered, I don't relish the trip. It means more explanations, too. Poor Giana, this must all be rather boring for you.'

'Not at all!' She said it eagerly, too eagerly perhaps for she thought Breid gave her an odd look. 'Where exactly are we going?'

'The Retreat is a place I own on the Norfolk Broads.'

'A holiday home?' Yet another establishment, she marvelled.

'Something like that,' he agreed. 'We—that is, Francesca and I—called it our retreat from the world— hence the name. It was our first real home of our own. We spent the first few years of our marriage in a small rented flat in the suburbs of London. I wasn't earning much in those days. I was only nineteen when we married.' He grimaced wryly. 'As I told you, I was a journalist for some years.' He was silent for such a long while that Giana finally prompted him.

'You said your wife was an artist?'

'Yes. When we met she was already making a name for herself. She was two years older than me,' he explained. 'The second year we were married we managed to afford a holiday on the Broads and Francesca fell in love with the area. Do you know it at all?'

'No. I haven't been to very many places. And I haven't had a holiday since I went on...' She stopped abruptly. She'd nearly said since her honeymoon in Jersey. 'We couldn't afford many family holidays,' she ended lamely.

'Francesca would have liked to live in Norfolk all year round. It wasn't possible of course, my work kept me in London, but the obsession stayed with her. She went up there several times by herself for a weekend's painting and after one trip she told me she'd bought us a second home. I hit the roof. I said we couldn't afford it, but it turned out she'd sold quite a few paintings and she'd hoarded the money for that purpose. I'm afraid I was a bit churlish about it at first. I didn't like the idea, you see, that she'd had to buy what she wanted for herself. I wanted to be the provider. But after that we spent every weekend we could manage doing the place up—and it certainly needed it. But it was fun.' The blue-grey eyes shone reminiscently. 'The place seemed more uniquely ours once we'd imposed our own personality on it. It *was* a unique place.'

For the first time since Giana had met him a real smile lit his face. Its effect upon her was startling. Her heart lurched in her breast like a thing gone crazy. But he'd forgotten all about *her*, Giana realised. His eyes, more cloudy grey than blue now, no longer saw the present scene. He was back in the early halcyon days of his marriage.

'When Tina was born we were glad we had somewhere other than a poky flat to spend weekends. The atmosphere seemed to inspire Francesca. She painted like a woman possessed. She sold more and more of her pictures. I began to work my way up until I was a senior reporter and we were able to move to a better flat. But we never gave up our country retreat.'

'I can understand,' Giana said softly, 'why you resent your daughter and...and Anthony Leyburn using the place for their...'

'Yes, I do resent it. Bitterly.' Her words had returned him to the present with a jolt. The smile vanished and he went on heavily, 'Sometimes Francesca would spend weeks at a time there, touring her beloved Broads and painting.'

'Did you mind her going off on her own?' Anthony had objected to the long hours Giana worked. Not, she now suspected, because he had missed her but because her absence detracted from his creature comforts.

'I missed her, of course. But marriage shouldn't be a straitjacket. She had a life of her own to carve out and I was proud of her talent. She just been accepted as a member of the Royal Academy when...' He stopped short, his eyes blank with a dreadful anguish.

'Was she ill?' Giana asked gently and was startled when he looked at her as if she were mad. Or as if he were mad, perhaps, for his eyes were wide and lit with a steely glare.

'Ill? No! I think I might have coped with that. Everyone is vulnerable to illness and we all have to die sooner or later according to the will of God. But I can't and won't accept the right of man to end another person's life.'

'You mean...' Some of the horror in his voice coloured Giana's breathless question. 'Was it...was it an accident?'

'Accident be damned!' He stood up and rested his arms on the overmantel, his head bowed so that he seemed to stare into the leaping flames. 'Francesca was murdered.' He was silent for a moment or two and Giana saw his strongly corded neck work convulsively. She dared not move nor speak. 'I don't know why I'm telling you all this,' he muttered at last. 'I haven't spoken of it to anyone in years.'

'But that hasn't helped, has it?' Giana ventured gently. 'It's always on your mind.'

'To all intents and purposes my life ended with Francesca's death,' he said simply. 'I began to wonder, not why I was on this earth, but what for.'

'It shows in your writing,' Giana told him. 'That's why your books never have happy endings. And the book you lent me to read, *Don't Ask Why*, the title is based on what you've just said. That was your wife's story, wasn't it? How you must hate whoever it was that killed her.'

'And my child!' He turned back towards her and Giana saw that he had his features well under control. His eyes, though bleak, were tearless. 'Francesca was six months pregnant . . . it would have been another girl. We thought we weren't going to have any more children. Tina was sixteen and away at boarding school.'

If Tina had been sixteen when her mother was killed, Giana calculated, then it was only three years since Breid had lost his wife—before she'd known Anthony. Breid had stopped speaking and Giana saw how difficult it was for him to go on.

'What happened?' she prompted.

'Two men broke in one night and ransacked the place. Francesca must have woken up and gone downstairs. At the trial one of the men admitted he hit her. He swore he didn't mean to kill her but the pathologist said she had a thin skull. The brute got away with manslaughter.'

'No wonder you dread going back to Norfolk. Have you been since...?'

'No. I bought the manor at Dinas Mead instead. It didn't have any memories. And yet I can't bring myself to sell The Retreat. The idea of anyone else living there... Heaven knows what sort of a state it'll be in.' He looked at Giana. 'Still want to come? I shan't blame you if you don't.'

'I'll come with you,' she told him quietly.

He leant forward across the space between the chesterfields and for an instant his hand brushed hers.

'You were right when you said you were a good listener. And you have a compassionate nature. Thank you for listening, Giana. I'm beginning to think I've found a good friend in you, as well as an excellent secretary.' Then, as if he felt he had been betrayed into showing enough emotion for one day, his hand fell away and he stood abruptly. 'I think I'll turn in. We'll make an early start tomorrow. It's as well to get to The Retreat before dark, especially at this time of year.'

For an instant Giana felt herself unable to move. His revelations and now the touch of his hand on hers had stirred that longing within her once more. Giana was not naïve; she recognised the longing for what it was. But it was a longing that must be quelled. Either that or she must shun Breid Winterton's company. He'd spoken of friendship. He would be horrified if he so

much as guessed at her deeper reactions to him. She realised that he was still standing, looking at her expectantly. She took a deep, steadying breath and stood
up, moved towards the door.

'Goodnight.'

'Goodnight, Giana. Sleep well.'

But sleep was a long time coming as Giana fought
against the knowledge that she was deeply sexually attracted to Breid Winterton. That fact, combined with
her increasing liking for the man, made a dangerous
combination. For the sake of her integrity and peace of
mind she ought to hope that tomorrow's journey into
Norfolk would resolve his fears about his daughter's
safety and end the need for her own association with
Breid.

But that meant Giana must also hope they would find
Anthony and Tina together at The Retreat. And she
hadn't decided yet how she would cope with such an
eventuality. All she knew for the moment was that she
dreaded Breid's reaction when he knew how she had de-
ceived him.

Despite Breid's intentions, a series of telephone calls de-
layed their departure and it was mid-morning before they
left Makepeace Gardens.

Rain was falling with a steady monotony as the Rolls
Royce purred out of London en route for the East
Anglian countryside. Breid's mood seemed to reflect the
gloomy weather. He spoke very little and Giana respected his silence.

Their route took them through Chelmsford and Colchester, towns already known to Giana. But once they entered Suffolk she was in unfamiliar territory.

It was midday when they reached Ipswich. Once a timber-built town, it still retained a few timber-framed houses, and it was at one of these, converted into a café, that they made a brief stop for lunch. The café thronged with Saturday morning shoppers but they managed to secure a corner seat and a fresh-faced girl took their order.

'Have we much further to go?' Giana asked as they ate.

'About fifty miles. I thought we'd put up overnight at Ulfketle.'

'Ulfketle?' Giana exclaimed disbelievingly, and a rare smile illuminated Breid's face.

'The nearest village to The Retreat. Strange name, isn't it? Apparently it's named after an eleventh-century Earl of East Anglia. We shouldn't have any difficulty getting rooms at the Fisherman's Return.' Soberly, 'I wouldn't want to spend the night at The Retreat.'

'If your daughter and . . . and Anthony Leyburn have been using it, it must be habitable, surely?'

'Maybe!' Breid said curtly. 'But I still don't intend to stay there overnight.'

'Of course not. I do understand.'

'Do you?' Breid gave her what she'd come to think of as one of his odd looks. 'I'm not sure that you do, Giana.'

For some reason his words and his tone of voice made her feel uncomfortable. She changed the subject slightly.

'Do you think we'll find Tina and Anthony Leyburn at The Retreat?'

'Frankly I don't know what to expect. I'm amazed that Leyburn's had the gall to use the place as he has. But I don't suppose he's suffered a moment's conscience about what happened there.'

'Why should he?' Giana was puzzled by this strange remark and not a little uneasy.

Breid signalled to the waitress for their bill and they were out in the rainswept street before he answered her question.

'Because I hold him entirely to blame for the burglary and the attack on Francesca.'

'How? Why?' Shocked beyond belief, Giana stopped short. Her face pale and drawn, she stared up at Breid, heedless of the downpour.

'Because it was one of his damned sensational articles that drew attention to the fact that the place was worth burgling.' He took her elbow and hustled her towards the car. 'You're getting wet. Get in.' As he took his seat beside her he looked at her, a worried frown contorting his brow. 'Are you all right?' he said sharply.

The colour was back in her cheeks now. His unexpected concern and the way he was leaning towards her had combined to induce that rush of feeling that she was experiencing more and more frequently in his presence.

'I'm all right,' she told him a little unsteadily.

For what seemed a long time he continued to study her face. Then, in an abrupt movement, he put out a hand and brushed a wet strand of hair back from her face. As he did so his fingers brushed her cheek and for a moment seemed to linger, warm against her cool, damp flesh.

Giana sat there like someone stunned. She felt as if she had stopped breathing. Her heart seemed suspended in mid-beat. She was unaware of the widening of her hazel eyes as she stared into the blue-grey ones that seemed not so very far away, that seemed to her to come closer. For some reason her gaze transferred itself to his mouth. For once its lines were softened, the lower lip revealing a promise of sensuality. Giana wasn't quite sure afterwards whether she had made a movement towards him but with a sudden jerky movement he straightened and started the engine.

'There *is* a difference,' he said as if to himself. 'And Francesca's eyes were brown.'

Giana felt as if someone had hit her below the heart. While she, like a fool, had been falling under his sexual spell, Breid—because of an unfortunate resemblance—had merely been comparing her to his late wife. And finding *her* wanting, obviously.

For the next few miles she stared unseeingly ahead, trying to come to terms with what had happened to her. For the unforgivable had happened. Unforgivable because she was a married woman. It wasn't just a sexual attraction she felt. She'd fallen in love with Breid Winterton. She hadn't realised it until just now, yet all the signs had been there. She had liked him from the start and her body had recognised its need long ago, before she'd been ready to make the mental admission.

The whole thing was a mess, she thought wearily. Her entire upbringing, all her values, were against any chance of sorting it out. True to her parents' teaching, she believed wholeheartedly that divorce was wrong. And even if she could convince herself that Anthony's behaviour released her from any moral obligation to him, Breid Winterton was still irrevocably wedded to memories of his dead wife.

They were in Norfolk now, the road signs informed her. It was a pity she was seeing this part of the country for the first time under such circumstances and in such weather. Had things been different she would have enjoyed seeing the charming villages, many of them predominantly built of flint. Their hard, speckled, almost 'tweedy' texture lent the whole countryside a distinctive character.

All too soon for Breid, Giana suspected, they reached the turning off the main road, signposted 'Ulfketle'.

A mile or so further on the road wound through a valley following the line of a river which, because of the rain, had overflowed its banks in places, flooding the low-lying meadows.

'It doesn't look much now,' Breid said, 'but it's beautiful here in summer. Francesca always used to say if Constable had been born at Ulfketle instead of East Bergholt, the River Thurne would have been as famous as the Stour.'

Ulfketle was no larger than Dinas Mead. Low-lying, surrounded by watery fields, it was a scattered lost place, an amphibious never-never land. The inn, the Fisherman's Return, stood by the river bridge. Giana stayed in the car while Breid booked rooms.

'No point in unpacking our luggage now,' he told her. They had only a suitcase each. 'We can take them in after we've been out to The Retreat.'

The continuation of the road took them further and further from any kind of civilisation. They were in the Broads proper now, a land where the difference in level between land and water was only a few inches. In some cases not even this difference existed.

'It's because of all the rain we've had,' Breid explained. 'Once upon a time all this area would have been open to navigation.'

The land itself consisted of flooded reed beds and alder swamps. Mysterious little channels opened off the river and widened out into tree-surrounded lakes. The flat horizon of the countryside was softened by occasional far oases of farms.

The road wound and narrowed and at last, when it seemed impossible they could drive any further, the car bumped across a bridge over a disused lock overhung by willow trees and took what was scarcely more than a muddy track through the marshes.

'There it is! The Retreat!' Despite his reluctance to come here, Breid's voice held a note of affection.

Through the streaming windscreen Giana peered where he pointed.

'Good heavens! It's a windmill!'

'Of course. Didn't I tell you?'

He certainly hadn't.

The white windmill with its black turret stood on a fifty-yard strip of green that rose slightly above marshes that stretched away beyond the eye's discerning. There was a small area of concrete in front of the mill that did duty as a hardstand, and here Breid parked the Rolls. There were no other cars. If Tina and Anthony had been at The Retreat, it didn't look as if they were here now.

'The mill was only a shell when Francesca bought it,' Breid explained. 'That's why she was able to get it so cheaply.'

'It certainly looks an unlikely spot for burglars,' Giana couldn't help remarking as she got out of the car.

'So it would have been...' He selected a key from a bunch in his hand. '...if it hadn't been for our friend Leyburn and the gratis information about the contents.'

'But why should he be so interested in you and Francesca?' she asked as he motioned her to precede him through the door. She twisted her fair head around to look at Breid. 'He goes in for the more sensational kind of journalism—scandal about well-known people. Surely you and...?'

'What journalists can't find they invent,' he said bitterly. 'But how do you know so much about Leyburn's work?' The question was rapped out.

To her everlasting credit, Giana thought, her wits did not desert her. In the tiny hallway she turned to face him.

'It's only what I've gathered from the things you've said about him.' She waited nervously. Would he accept her explanation?

For a moment he held her gaze, then gave a grunt which could have meant anything. He brushed past her and Giana was acutely aware of a nerve-tingling contact at thigh and shoulder before he led the way into the mill proper.

'Oh!' Giana gasped. 'It's not a bit like I expected.'

'Take a look round if you like,' Breid invited. With the pull of a single cord a vast system of oatmeal-coloured blinds swung open to reveal a large picture-window and let in the grey afternoon light.

The ground floor consisted of an enormous lounge. Giana calculated that the diameter must be around thirty feet. Though a fine layer of dust covered the modern wooden furnishings and the beautiful parquet floor, it could not disguise the room's functional elegance. Further investigation revealed an L-shaped extension which had not been visible from the front of the mill. This formed a kitchen and dining area as well as a spacious apartment which had obviously been used as an artist's studio. Pictures, mostly landscapes, some half-finished, still lined its walls. An easel, canvases and paints had been left just as they must have been when Francesca Winterton last used them.

'There's a bedroom on each of the other four floors,' Breid told her, 'each with its own private bathroom.'

'There's no one here,' Giana pointed out somewhat unnecessarily. She realised she was relieved at not having to face Anthony, but even more relieved that she need not yet reveal her true identity to Breid.

'No.' Breid was investigating the contents of the refrigerator. 'But someone has been some time in the last few weeks. The electricity's switched on.' He sniffed at the contents of a milk bottle and wrinkled his nose. 'Sour.'

There were other signs of recent occupancy. The kitchen cupboards held packet and tinned foods. Lipstick-stained cigarette stubs filled a brass ashtray. An empty cigarette carton which Giana recognised as the brand Anthony smoked lay on a table. He disdained her dislike of the habit, her repeated concern over health warnings. Giana was glad Breid didn't smoke. She hated working in a tobacco-filled atmosphere and found the acrid tang it gave to the hair and clothes of smokers distinctly unpleasant.

At Breid's invitation Giana followed him up the winding staircase, a carpenter's masterpiece, beautifully crafted in pitchpine. Giana marvelled at the ingenuity of the bedrooms. All interior design had had to be determined by the circular nature of the building. Everywhere there were little treasures of craftsmanship, such as an irregularly-shaped and curved door made of pine, each slat cut on the curve so that the door filled its tiny space exactly.

Two of the rooms had double beds. For Breid's sake Giana hoped Tina Winterton had had the sensitivity not to use her parents' room for her illicit relationship with Anthony Leyburn. She saw Breid's lips tighten when one room showed signs of dual occupancy. He said nothing, however, and Giana felt it could not have been the one he had shared with Francesca; for surely that would have provoked an explosion of wrath.

'I suppose this windmill's quite old?' Giana asked. The interior décor had made much use of the original brickwork which, Breid told her, had merely been repointed.

'Yes. Francesca researched its history. There's been a windmill on this site since the middle of the eighteenth century.' In 1860, he explained, the mill had been converted from wind power to steam. 'But then, shortly afterwards, the boiler blew up and set the place on fire. The interior collapsed and it was never used again except by itinerant wildfowl until Francesca bought it. What do you think of the place?' he asked.

'It's perfectly splendid.' It was a beautiful building, Giana thought, and it had obviously been lovingly restored to the highest standard of craftsmanship. 'And such a novel idea. I would never have thought of living in a windmill.'

'Francesca had a true artist's vision.' A jealousy she had no right to feel twisted Giana's heart as he spoke affectionately of his wife.

'Even when it was at its worst,' he went on, 'full of bird droppings and nests where the joists should have been, she saw its potential.'

Giana thrust unworthy thoughts away and concentrated on their conversation.

'It must have been hard work.'

'It was. We had to have some professional help, naturally. The structure had to be strengthened and different floors put in. All the windows were at the wrong level, since it was never intended as a home. I bricked those up myself and made the new openings. But I'm sorry, Giana,' he apologised. 'You must find all this terribly boring.'

'Not a bit,' she told him earnestly, then wistfully, 'I've often thought I'd like to do a place up from scratch. It must be very satisfying.'

Breid looked at her approvingly, she thought.

'Would you like to see our "view"?' he asked.

The 'view' was from the roof. Access was gained via a hatchway on the fourth floor, which led out on to a small platform, some sixty-five feet above ground level. It was still raining, a thin, fine drizzle now which obscured the view he spoke of. But on a clear day, Breid said, one could see for miles across the vast expanse of Broadland.

'It's a marvellous place for bird-watching,' Breid said as they stood shoulder to shoulder in the small enclosed space.

'You like doing that?'

'It used to be a hobby of mine when I stayed here regularly. I don't suppose living in a place like this would appeal to you very much?' he asked.

'Oh, I don't know,' Giana contradicted. 'I haven't always been a city dweller and surely,' her voice was suddenly husky, 'it depends who you share a place with? There's something...' She hesitated, wondering if he would think her foolish, then, 'there's something very romantic about the idea of living in a windmill. It's rather like an inland lighthouse, isn't it? A beacon for miles around in all this flat countryside.'

'Yes.' Breid had been watching the earnest lines of her profile. 'In good weather we could see it from miles away and know that home was in sight. It was a good feeling.' He cleared his throat suddenly and looked at his watch. 'Time we were getting back to the Fisherman before the light goes. In flood conditions like this it would be easy to lose the track and land the car in several feet of water.' He preceded her through the hatchway then proferred a helping hand.

Unthinkingly, Giana took it. She was totally unprepared for the sudden rush of sensation she experienced as their palms met and she stepped through the aperture to find herself breast to breast with Breid, so close that she could detect a tantalising odour of masculine cologne and feel his warm breath on her forehead. Startled into unwariness, she looked up at him, almost in protest against this sudden assault on her feelings. She met his gaze and began to tremble, aware that her eyes were revealing too much.

She tried to snatch away her hand but found his grip too strong, suddenly painfully so.

'Giana?' He said her name on a questioning note. 'What is it?'

'N-nothing. It's all right.'

'But you're shaking.'

'I'm cold,' she improvised quickly. 'It must have been the damp out there.'

'Is that all?' He sounded doubtful. 'I thought perhaps...' He shrugged. Then, 'In that case we'll get back to the inn as quickly as possible. You'd better have a hot bath. I hope you haven't caught a chill.'

What ailed her was far more serious than that, Giana thought miserably. And seeing the home he'd built and shared with Francesca, a home still impregnated with fond memories, had only underlined the impossibility of her own love for Breid Winterton. Her eyes smarted suddenly and her throat ached.

It was on the first downward flight of stairs that the accident happened. Her eyes misted with tears, Giana stumbled. She had already regained her balance when Breid turned, but in doing so he lost his own. The damp soles of his shoes failed to find their grip and he fell heavily, thudding headfirst down several of the spiral-built stairs before he came to rest against the curving wall, one foot bent unnaturally under him.

White-faced, Giana took the stairs at a run and dropped down on her knees beside him.

'Breid!' It was the first time she'd used his name. Until now she'd successfully avoided calling him anything. Mr Winterton seemed too formal, but he hadn't invited her to use his first name. 'Oh, Breid, are you all right?'

To her horror he didn't answer and then she saw, where his forehead rested against the brick wall, a nasty bruise that was already beginning to swell.

'Breid! Oh, my God!' It was a choked cry of fear. There could be such dreadful results from an injury to the head.

Somehow she stumbled into the nearest bedroom, into its en suite bathroom. Investigation of a cupboard revealed a neat pile of unused face flannels. She ran a tap until the water ran icy cold, soaked the flannel, then hurried back to where Breid still lay. With shaking hands she pressed the makeshift compress to his injury.

'Oh, please, let him be all right, please.' She didn't realise she was praying aloud.

After a moment or two—to Giana it seemed like hours—he stirred, his eyelids flickered, then opened. Unfocused at first, grey-blue eyes stared hazily up at Giana.

'Fran?' he murmured.

Oh, this was the giddy limit. First he frightened the life out of her, then he mistook her for his wife. Damn this unfortunate likeness she bore to Francesca Winterton! Giana made to scramble to her feet but a groan from Breid as he straightened his leg stayed her hasty movement.

'Dammit! I think I've broken something. And that fall must have knocked me out. For a minute I couldn't think where I was. I'm sorry, Giana, for a second there I took you for Francesca.'

'I wish I had been!' she said impulsively, then added quickly, 'For your sake, I mean. For... for a while...' her voice wobbled '...I thought you were dead.'

There was nothing wrong with his vision now. A comprehensive glance took in her pallor, the way she was trembling, the silent tears of relief that spilled down her cheeks. The next moment she was in his arms and she clung to him, her face buried against his chest.

'It's all right, Giana, love,' he soothed. 'I'm very far from dead.'

How she treasured that word 'love', though he'd meant nothing by it.

He held her until the shaking subsided. His touch on her hair was comforting, soothing, and involuntarily she gave a little murmur of pleasure. She knew she ought to move away but something stronger than that knowledge held her mesmerised. His maleness was as potent as a drug.

It was only when he gave a faint groan that she withdrew herself from his arms.

'Breid, I'm sorry.' She dashed a hand across her eyes. 'You're in pain and here am I acting like an idiot. What must you think of me? I'm not usually such a fool.'

He was calmly understanding.

'It was a very natural reaction. But if you're OK now, I think I'd better move.'

'Let me help you up.' Anxiously, 'Can you stand?'

'I'm not sure.' He grimaced. 'But I'll try.'

As he struggled to rise, his arm about Giana's shoulders, hers about his waist, she fought to concentrate on the task in hand rather than on his nearness, her quivering reactions to it.

As his injured foot touched the stair she felt him wince, heard his sharp intake of breath.

'It's bad, isn't it?'

''Fraid so. I don't think I'm going to make it down all those stairs yet. If you could help me hobble as far as the bedroom...'

It was a slow, painful progress. To Giana, sensitive to the pain Breid must be feeling, it seemed to take ages before he lowered himself on to the bed.

'Here, let me.' She unfastened his laces and eased the shoe and sock from a foot that was already swollen and discoloured. 'That looks nasty. You're going to need a doctor. Maybe even an X-ray. I think I'd better phone...'

'The telephone's been cut off for the past three years. And there's no doctor in Ulfketle.'

'Maybe not, but there's a phone at the inn. If you'll trust me with your car I'll...'

'It's not a question of trust,' Breid said wearily. 'It would be far too dangerous for you. Look out of the window.'

Giana did so. In the time it had taken for Breid to regain consciousness and for her to help him into the bedroom, the short winter afternoon was over. Darkness had come down over the marshes and with it fresh torrents of rain.

'But that means...'

'We're stuck here for the night,' Breid agreed. 'It's a good thing we didn't leave our suitcases at the

Fisherman.' Despite the pain he must be suffering, he essayed a wry grin. 'Don't look so worried, Giana.'

'But I am worried, about your foot. It needs attention.'

'Agreed. And if you'd be kind enough to make another of your very efficient compresses I'd be most grateful. You never know, it may be just a sprain. By morning I may be able to get downstairs.'

Over the next hour Giana repeatedly applied cold compresses to Breid's ankle. The swelling did not seem appreciably improved but he swore it was more comfortable for her ministrations.

'You're wasted as a secretary,' he teased. 'You ought to be in a more caring profession...' Giana started nervously as he went on. 'A nurse, maybe.' If only he knew! Then, more seriously, he said, 'You'd make a wonderful wife and mother. I can't think why some man hasn't snapped you up yet. Have you never contemplated marriage, Giana?'

She flushed and stammered out some kind of reply, scarcely aware of what she said and with a desperate need to change the subject.

'If you'll give me your keys I'll get our cases out of the car. And then I suppose I'd better see if I can rustle up a meal. There must be something suitable among that stuff in the kitchen.'

It was eerie being alone outside. A strong wind had risen and lashed the steadily falling rain against the stout walls of the windmill. Head down, Giana struggled against its force, then, herded by the wind's strength, had almost to run back inside with the suitcases.

'I'm afraid it's a very rudimentary meal,' she told Breid apologetically when half an hour later she carried a laden tray into his bedroom. 'Only boiled rice and some tinned vegetable curry.'

'It smells great,' he assured her. 'I'm only sorry you had to toil all the way up those stairs with it. If I had to fall it's a pity it wasn't nearer the ground floor.'

Peaches and tinned custard completed their meal and when they'd finished eating Giana began to stack the dishes back on the tray.

'Leave those for now,' Breid said. 'Stay and talk to me for a bit.' It was an odd request considering he'd been silently thoughtful all through the meal.

'Talk? What about?'

'Mainly about your future plans. I know it's been rather an odd beginning to your employment, and perhaps it's too soon to tell, but do you think you're going to like working for me, Giana?' He paused, then, 'Can we consider it a permanent arrangement?'

CHAPTER FIVE

'WELL, Giana,' as she didn't answer immediately. '*Will* you stay?'

But she couldn't stay. She had a job to go back to, in just two weeks, and a husband whom Breid must never know about. If he ever found out why, in the first place, she'd entered his employ... Giana shuddered. With the loaded tray in her hand, she edged towards the door.

'I... You said I was on a month's trial,' she fenced.

An impatient movement of his hand waved her objection aside.

'I think we both know you've more than proved your worth to me.'

Giana's heartbeat increased and she took a deep breath to steady it. If she were foolish enough to do so, she could easily misinterpret that remark.

'A month's trial works both ways,' she pointed out.

'I see!' Thoughtfully the blue-grey eyes scanned her slightly flushed face. 'Am I to take it you don't like working for me? These last two weeks haven't been typical, you know. Give it a bit longer, Giana, hmm?' Then, with a touch of irritation, 'For heaven's sake put down that damned tray. Come and sit over here where I can see you properly.' A peremptory hand indicated the edge of his bed and reluctantly Giana obeyed. 'What exactly is it you don't care for?' he asked. 'Is it the isolation at Dinas Mead? You wouldn't be the first to object to that. You're young, so I suppose you still find the city lights alluring. Suppose I said I'd do all my work at the London house? Would you be prepared to stay on then?'

'Did you ever suggest that to your other secretaries?' Giana couldn't repress her curiosity.

'No.' He said it gravely, his eyes intent on her face.

'Then why...?' She regretted the impulsive question and her voice trailed away before his quizzical look. There was a long silence before he said, as though it were dragged from him against his will,

'Because I find I don't want to lose *you*.'

Giana's face flamed anew. She looked at Breid uncertainly. Sometimes it was impossible to fathom his expression. He couldn't mean... No, that was impossible. A dangerous notion to conceive. She tried to cover her reactions with a laugh. It came out rather shakily.

'That's quite some compliment to my secretarial abilities. At least it sounds as if I can count on a good reference.' Instead of deflecting him from his purpose, her laugh had the opposite effect.

'Damn your secretarial abilities!' Breid exploded. 'And damn giving you a reference! For all I care you could type with two fingers. I told you, it's *you* I want to hang on to, not just a secretary.'

His words left Giana totally bereft of speech. She simply gazed at him, her hazel eyes enormous in her heart-shaped face, while her pulses raced erratically.

Breid shifted restlessly on the bed as though he would move towards her, but a sudden spasm of pain contorted his face.

'Blast this ankle!' he muttered. Then, with a wry glance at Giana's troubled expression, 'I haven't exactly chosen an auspicious moment to start this conversation, have I? I'm in pain and you're tired out. You've been toiling up and down all those stairs while I've been lying here like a useless hulk. We'll talk about it again in the morning.'

'I don't...' Giana began as she stood up, but he interrupted her.

'In the morning,' he told her firmly. 'Now, better pick yourself a bedroom. You won't be nervous on your own? I don't think we'll be troubled by intruders on a night like this.'

'Were you burgled more than once then?' Giana wasn't generally of a nervous disposition but The Retreat was so isolated and it had been the target of violence before.

'Only the once. Once was enough! Now, you're sure you're not afraid of being alone? If so, you could stay up here with me...'

'Oh, no!' she said hastily, too hastily, for his eyes narrowed shrewdly. 'I'll be perfectly all right.' She snatched up the tray and hurried towards the door, even though she knew Breid was physically incapable right now of restraining her.

'Giana!' On the threshold she halted and gave him a wary glance, but he hadn't moved. 'Think about what I said. Don't make any decisions until we've had time to talk it through, but think about it, hmm?'

A coherent answer was impossible. She made a sound in her throat that could have meant anything, then hurried away down the spiralling staircase to the kitchen.

She was amazed that her shaking legs still had the strength to get her there.

She wasn't going to think about it, she told herself as she prepared for bed in the room just below Breid's. There was nothing to think about. Yet how she loved Breid, she brooded longingly. God alone knew how much she loved him, but she couldn't stay with him—in any capacity—and that was that, no matter how much pain the knowledge cost her. She was going to get a good night's sleep. Then, in the morning, she would tell him, politely but firmly, that she'd work out her month but then she was leaving. After all, she'd found out what she had set out to discover—why Breid was having Anthony followed. His reasons weren't sinister but perfectly reasonable ones. He could track down his daughter and sort her out without Giana's help. With luck he need never know she was Anthony's wife.

As for Anthony, when he came home, which he must do some time if only to collect his belongings, his affair with Tina Winterton might have burnt itself out. Giana wasn't sure how she would face him with her knowledge of his behaviour, but she did know what her father would say. The Reverend Spencer would tell her it was her bounden duty to forgive and forget her husband's faults and peccadilloes and try to make her marriage work. And Giana was sufficiently her father's daughter to believe he was right. That, she thought wryly, was exactly what she'd been doing anyway for the second six months of her year-long marriage.

It was all very well to tell herself she was going to sleep soundly. Sleep was a recalcitrant visitor that night. Giana couldn't get Breid's words out of her head—'it's

you I don't want to lose'. It was just possible she'd misunderstood his meaning, but she didn't think so. There
had been something in the smoky gaze of his eyes far
more telling than mere words. Behind her determinedly
closed eyelids, his lean face, framed by the silvered blond
hair, took shape as clearly as if her eyes beheld the
original.

Breid's wife had been dead three years. In life's span
that was a relatively short time, but in terms of loss and
loneliness it must have seemed much longer. Breid might
be ready to emerge from his emotionally crippled state
and if she, Giana, had been the catalyst stirring him into
new life, she knew she didn't want to be the means of
hurting him, of making him retreat into his limbo again.
Which was another reason why she must leave him as
soon as possible. Any attraction he felt towards her could
only be a dawning one as yet, but if they were together
any longer it might deepen and become intolerable for
both of them.

Giana was usually totally honest with herself. But on
this occasion she tried to ignore the fact that, for her,
it was already too late.

Still too restless to settle, she looked around for something to read. This usually had the desired soporific
effect. There were no books but in the bedside cupboard
she found a pile of glossy magazines. They were several
years old, of course, but that didn't matter. She selected
the most recent and recognised as she did so that it was
the Sunday colour supplement to the paper Anthony
worked for. Being already familiar with its style, she was
about to discard it in favour of another publication when

a picture inset on the cover caught her attention—the photograph of a windmill.

Quickly she turned to the contents page. 'Murgatroyd's Retreat—But is it?', she read. She checked the page number then flicked through the magazine. In the centre a full-page spread confronted her. The left-hand page showed a woman, Francesca Winterton, standing outside The Retreat. She was unmistakably pregnant. Beside her, standing with the ungainly self-consciousness of youth, was a dark-haired girl. The face was three years younger, but Giana recognised her. The girl was the one to whom Anthony had paid so much attention at the Pratts' party. The utter gall of it! He'd actually had an assignation with Tina Winterton right under his wife's very nose, she thought furiously. And this was the man on whose behalf *she* was having scruples. It was a few minutes before she could bring herself to study the rest of the feature.

The right-hand page and the pages that followed showed shots of the interior of the windmill, and Giana could see what Breid had meant when he said the intruders had had their homework done for them.

The rooms were as she, Giana, knew them now, but the contents were vastly different. Glowing Old Masters hung on the walls, antique silver adorned sideboard and dresser. A close-up of a glass-topped table showed a display of valuable miniatures.

She turned her attention to the written text. In every word she could hear Anthony's voice, light, sarcastic, cleverly insinuating. He managed to make Breid's wonderful novels sound second-rate and superficial. He implied that all was not as it seemed with Breid and

Francesca Winterton's marriage, that both had been seen with other partners—Breid in the city, Francesca in her Norfolk haunts. The photographs and his description of their converted windmill were merely background to his scurrilous search for scandal. Even though Giana was familiar with her husband's style of journalism, she was more than usually sickened by the feature, hating what Anthony had done to Breid Winterton and his family.

She thrust the magazine out of sight back in the cupboard, switched off the bedside light and resigned herself to sleeplessness, so it took her by surprise when light streaming through the uncurtained window woke her to a new day.

It hadn't stopped raining, she observed as, having showered, she pulled on fresh jeans and a green sweater which gave her hazel eyes the illusory depth of twin emeralds. The sweater was rather tight around her generously proportioned breasts but it was the warmest she had with her and the morning air struck a damp chill, even through the mill's sturdy walls. When she was working usually she tied her silvery blonde tresses back from her face in a convenient ponytail, but her present situation was hardly a workaday one, so this morning she let her hair fall loose about her face and ripple over her shoulders in a silken cascade. This way, she found, it made a convenient veil for her emotions, and she might well have need of concealing them today.

She wasn't looking forward to her next encounter with Breid. Perhaps, she encouraged herself, in the cool light of day he would have changed his mind about what he'd intended to say last night. Yet somehow that thought, too, displeased her. Light of foot but heavy-hearted she ran downstairs to see what the kitchen could offer in the way of breakfast. Where the last flight of stairs curved into the living area she came to an abrupt halt.

'What on earth are you doing down here?'

Breid was already ensconced on a large comfortable settee, his foot resting on a stool. He greeted her cheerfully.

'The ankle's a lot better this morning. It's obviously not broken after all.'

'Oh, good! That means we'll be able to leave. If you'll let me drive?' Although Giana knew she was a careful, skilful motorist, Anthony never allowed her to drive when they went out together.

''Fraid not!'

'Why not?' she demanded indignantly. 'I promise not to dent your precious car.'

'I didn't mean I wouldn't let you drive. I meant we're not leaving.'

'Why?' she asked suspiciously. Panic surged in her stomach. Then, with more confidence than she felt, 'You can't force me to stay.'

His features broke up into that smile she had seen so rarely and it had its usual instantaneous effect upon her fluttering nerves. It was more than a smile this time; it was a positive grin of amusement.

'What a suspicious mind you have. Look outside. Go on, open the front door and look.'

Giana did so. What she saw caused her to gasp in dismay. She realised, too, what a fool she'd made of herself. The torrential, persistent rain had flooded the dykes and tributaries of the River Thurne. Water had spread out over the flat surrounding countryside and, despite the mill's elevated position, now lapped inches deep at the very doorstep of The Retreat. She turned back towards Breid.

'I'm sorry,' she said stiffly. 'I thought...'

'Quite understandably.' Breid was amazingly affable this morning, even now, after she'd practically accused him of... 'It *is* rather a Gothic situation, isn't it?' he went on. 'Young woman trapped in an isolated place with an older experienced man. It's all right, Giana.' He actually chuckled. 'The ankle's still a bit too tender for me to leap on you and have my wicked way with you.'

He made it sound so ridiculous that Giana found herself smiling responsively, her wide mouth with its long top lip curving upward in what was perhaps the first real smile she'd ever given him.

'You sound more cheerful than usual,' she couldn't help saying. 'I was afraid spending the night here might have depressed you.'

'I thought it might have done, too,' he said, grave once more, 'which is why I dreaded coming here. But it wasn't so bad after all. And this morning when I woke up I knew I was glad to be in the old place again.'

'So you won't sell it? You'll use it again?'

'That rather depends.'

On what? Giana wondered, but Breid wasn't saying. Instead he asked, 'How's the food situation? We may well be here for a couple of days. Do we starve through the siege?'

'It's not quite as bad as that.' She smiled again. She felt curiously light-hearted herself. As a condemned man must do when reprieved, she found herself thinking, and the thought sobered her. For she knew it was because *she* had been reprieved. Once they left here she would have to exert herself to quit Breid's employment, but they didn't have to leave the windmill today, perhaps not even tomorrow.

Tinned sausages and crispbreads didn't make an exactly *haute cuisine* breakfast, but Breid made no complaint, and Giana couldn't help reflecting how very different Anthony's reaction would have been.

'It's a pity I didn't bring my shorthand notebook with me,' she said as she cleared away. 'We could have got on with some work. Goodness knows how we're going to spend the time until the floods go down. There's no radio or television, is there?' Then she turned away quickly to hide an embarrassed blush. Because, if things had been different, she could have thought of an extremely pleasurable way of filling the hours here with Breid. Hours that would not have seemed unduly long.

'How do you think people spent their time before there was television and radio?' Breid's question, asked in an amused lazy drawl, seemed to follow the trend of her thoughts and Giana disappeared rapidly in the direction of the kitchen. 'We have books,' he called after her, 'and we have conversation. There must be plenty of topics we haven't discussed yet.'

And one in particular which she didn't want him to get around to.

'Did the TV and radio go in the burglary as well?' she asked from the safety of the kitchen.

'Yes. A hell of a lot of stuff went. Some of it I shan't bother to replace. There should be pictures somewhere of what it used to look like—in a copy of our "friend" Leyburn's article.'

'I've seen it.' The breakfast things cleared away, there was no excuse to linger at the sink and Giana returned to the living-room. She perched on the extreme edge of a chair. 'There was a copy in my bedroom.'

'You read all of it, I suppose?' And, as she nodded, 'I want you to know, Giana, that it was all lies. Francesca was never unfaithful to me, nor I to her. Because, necessarily, we spent a fair amount of time apart, stories sprang up...'

'It...it's none of my business.'

'Maybe. Nevertheless I want you to know.'

Giana couldn't think of any further reply to that and Breid seemed to have nothing more to say on the subject. So much for conversation, she thought in a silence which grew longer and, to her, uneasier.

'I meant what I said last night,' Breid said suddenly. 'I don't want to lose you, Giana. Have you thought any more about it?'

She couldn't face the piercing scrutiny of those blue-grey eyes. She jumped up and went to stare out of the window though there was nothing but the rain-sodden landscape.

'Not really,' she said untruthfully. Then, over her shoulder without looking at him, 'I don't like tying myself down for any length of time. I'd rather move on, vary my experience.' As it always did on the rare occasions when she had to make use of an expedient lie, her father's accusing face loomed before her. 'Tell the truth no matter what the cost,' she could hear him saying.

'But surely if you go from job to job it doesn't look too well on your record,' Breid said. 'How do you explain all these short-term employments?'

Giana, who had only ever held two different jobs in her life, hesitated, searching for a plausible answer. She wasn't aware that Breid had left the settee and limped over to stand behind her until he touched her arm. Then she swung round with a startled gasp, almost cata-pulting herself into his arms as she did so. She recovered herself immediately and took a nervous step backwards.

'You...you startled me. Should...should you be standing on that foot?'

'Since it got me down three flights of stairs,' he said drily, 'I don't think half a dozen steps more will matter.' Then, 'Look, Giana, let's stop fencing, shall we? We both know this isn't just a question of whether you want to go on working for me or not.'

'Do we?' The motif on his sweater had a sudden ab-sorbing interest for her, anything rather than meet his eyes, and he gave an exasperated sigh.

'You know damned well what I'm getting at. Look——' he took hold of her arm and drew her after him towards the settee '—let's sit down. The ankle's OK when I walk, but standing still on it doesn't seem to be a very good idea.' He sat and pulled her down beside him, then he grasped her shoulders so that she had to face him. At his nearness, quivering warmth erupted in the lower half of Giana's body. Her gaze was drawn to his as if he had her hypnotised.

'Please, Breid, don't.' She didn't want him to put any-thing into words. While it remained unsaid she could pretend this sense of mutual magnetic attraction was all in her imagination. Once he had spoken it would be that much harder to go away and forget about him, as she must.

'It has to be said, Giana,' he told her seriously. 'True, I've only known you two weeks, but it seems longer. Already you've made a difference in my life. These last three years I've been living under a black cloud. And I've realised recently it's thanks to you that that cloud has begun to lift.'

'It would probably have lifted anyway,' she told him, dry-mouthed. 'You were probably ready to start living again anyway. It was just coincidence that I . . .'

'Coincidence nothing!' he snorted. 'Are you trying to tell me that anyone else would have done as well? Because *I'm* telling *you* that just isn't so.' His hands left her shoulders and came up to capture her face, shaping it, his thumbs smoothing the soft flesh over the high cheekbones, stained now with hectic colour. His eyes were dark with unmistakable sexual awareness.

'Then it's because I look like your wife,' she urged desperately, frightened because her body was responding even though her mind repudiated what was happening. 'You said once that you'd tried to imagine I *was* her.'

'Tried and failed,' he retorted. 'Oh, superficially you're like her.' One fingertip traced the outlines of her mouth, his eyes intently following the path of the finger's movement. 'You have the same bone-structure and the same colouring, but character doesn't have a carbon copy. In character you're totally unalike.'

She wanted to ask him what differences he'd found between her and Francesca, but she knew she mustn't let this conversation go on. She swallowed convulsively.

'We've been thrown together these last few days, in unusual circumstances. You said yourself they were unusual...'

'Stop it, Giana!' He said it almost savagely. 'Stop insulting my intelligence. Stop making excuses for me. I don't need them. I *know* how I feel.'

'All right! But,' with an attempt at defiance, 'you don't know how *I* feel.'

'I don't know,' he said slowly, 'but I have my ideas. I know what I'd like to think.' He subjected her to one of his long lingering scrutinies. Again the dark irises of his eyes were large and velvety so that their colour seemed to have deepened. Then, 'And theories have to be tested before proven.'

Mesmerised by his gaze, by the husky timbre of his voice, she guessed his intention a second too late.

'No, Breid, no!'

But she was already a captive in the hard band of his arms, engulfed by the heat of his body, by the male scent of him, warm and faintly musky. She wanted to reject him, to pull away, but the touch of his mouth, initially fleeting, questioning, testing, aroused a storm of need in her that seemed almost out of proportion to the caress. Sensual warmth flooded her veins as the exploratory kiss became more demanding. She must put a stop to this, Giana thought hazily, but pressed back against the settee it was impossible to move her head, and her hands, trapped between the two of them, thrust fruitlessly at Breid's chest as she tried to free herself.

The pressure of his mouth on hers increased, the hungry, demanding impact electrifying her. Pleasure that was almost pain lanced through her veins and beneath her suddenly slackened hands his heart thudded heavily. Then his tongue was painting lightly persuasive strokes of sensuality against her mouth, coaxing, imploring it to open to him. It was impossible, she found, not to respond to his kiss, to the sexual chemistry he sparked off inside her body.

As her lips parted to his she felt the vanquishing thrust of his tongue, heard the deep growl of male satisfaction in his throat.

He pulled her closer, one hand now cupping the eager, urgent, aching globes that her breasts had become. The thick wool of her sweater was an irksome barrier; she wanted to know his touch on her skin.

Hardly knowing what she did, Giana let her hands slide up over his shoulders until they found the taut, straining muscles of his neck. Her fingers caressed, plunged deeply in the thick hair at the nape and he pushed her more deeply into the settee, his weight imprisoning her, making her intimately aware of his arousal.

His hands had found the welt of her sweater now and slid up beneath it. He found and released the front fastening of her bra and a little moan of ecstasy escaped her as his fingers found the flesh that already yearned for more intimate contact.

He was impatient with the thick wool of the sweater now, pushing it up so that his mouth could follow where his hands had led, and her entire body pulsated, sensation after sensation convulsing her as his lips brushed her soft skin and his tongue drew fiery whorls around the hardened, thrusting tips of her breasts. Her every nerve-end seemed concentrated on the intense pleasure he was arousing and there was a raw, wanting need inside her. It was she now who urged a greater closeness, arching her body against him in wanton, shuddering demand. But as sanity threatened to slip away from her entirely he released her mouth, though retaining his hold on her.

'Giana?' Her name was a husky, almost anxious question as he tried to gauge her expression. The look in his eyes made her shiver convulsively, wanting him to go on making love to her. But she knew that mustn't happen.

'I...I wish you hadn't done that,' she told him unsteadily.

It wasn't the vehement protest she should have made, she realised, but it was the best she could do in her shaken condition. She saw his expression clear.

'You don't really mean that,' he said confidently, and she knew he was about to kiss her again.

'Yes, Breid, I do mean it.' She should have had more pride than to indulge in casual dalliance with a man she barely knew, a man whose employ she would be leaving in a matter of weeks. And this time her words succeeded in holding him at bay.

'Why, love?' The words were spoken tenderly. 'It wasn't that bad, was it? In fact I got the distinct impression you were enjoying it. As for me,' he went on before she could frame a denial, 'it's a long, long time since I felt this way. Oh, Giana,' huskily, 'you're like a long sweet draught of water to a man who's been in an arid desert far too long.' His voice became unsteady. 'And I want you, Giana. God knows how I want you.'

He pressed his body to hers again and she could not doubt the truth of his words.

'Please don't say things like that,' she begged him, lips quivering. With emotions heightened, longings unfulfilled, she was not far from tears. 'You mustn't.'

'But I must say it,' he insisted, 'because it's true. Not only have you woken me from a long dark nightmare, but you've awoken needs in me that I believed to be dead, buried in Francesca's grave. I never thought to want anyone so much again.'

It wasn't fair. He aroused all her emotions, emotions that ranged from fierce feminine desire to an almost maternal compassion. And she wished with all her heart that it hadn't happened. She mustn't get any more involved with him. Already she'd allowed him intimacies which before had been permitted to her husband alone. A husband who didn't deserve her loyalty, an insidious inner voice whispered. She sought to stifle that voice. She fought against the desire to wrap her arms around Breid and give him all the love and affection that swelled within her breast, making both heart and body ache for its release.

'Please, Giana, let me make love to you.' He didn't wait for her answer, but despite his still tender ankle stood suddenly, pulling her with him, the better to hold her close against his pulsating body, intensifying the nagging ache deep inside her. His hand at her waist imprisoned the lower half of her body against his hips. The other hand cupped her chin, turning her mouth up to his. 'Don't deny me, Giana, not now. I need you.'

Heaven knew how wantonly she yearned for his more intimate possession. But it wasn't possible. She was a married woman. Married, yes, but to a man who had broken the vows of faithfulness he'd made to her, her flesh argued with her mind. But again the spectre of her father rose to chide her. 'Two wrongs don't make a right.'

'No, Breid, I can't. We mustn't.'

'Why not?' It was a persuasive murmur against her lips. 'We're both over twenty-one, both free.' Oh, the irony of it. 'What's to prevent us?'

'Me!' she said. 'I . . .'

'Are you a virgin, Giana?' He asked softly. Then, reassuringly, 'Because if so, I promise you . . .'

'No!'

'No, you're not a virgin or no, you won't let me . . . ?'

'Both!' she said a little wildly. But even then his persistence would not be checked.

'It doesn't matter, you know, that you're not a virgin. Your past isn't my concern. In fact,' his thigh muscles bunched against hers, 'it will make it so much easier. We can pleasure each other without any fear of . . .'

'No!' she said again, more urgently this time. 'Will you just get it into your head that when I say no, I mean no?'

'Then why let me go this far?' He was angry now, with the anger of frustrated desire. 'Your body's whole reaction tells me you want me as much as I want you.'

He had a right to feel cheated, to feel angry. Giana fought for self control.

'I'm sorry if I gave you the wrong impression.' She said it so quietly that the man watching her had no idea of the effort it cost her to deny her own feelings. She tried a placatory smile. 'You . . . you're an attractive man, you must know that, and . . .' she swallowed, 'and physically attractive. For a moment I let myself be carried away, but,' firmly, 'it's not what I want.'

His anger had not lessened his desire, nor had her denial. If anything his body was more urgent against her.

'If you've made love before, and you say you have, you must know how painful it is to come this far and be denied. Giana,' his grasp tightened, 'don't you realise how long it's been since I...? God, Giana, I *need* you! And I could have sworn you... I can't believe you mean what you say. Don't torment me.' His hoarse voice broke off and he buried his face in her hair.

She was glad he couldn't see her expression. Giana felt as though she were drowning in inwardly shed tears. She couldn't bear his anguish. In destroying him, if he but knew it, she was destroying herself. Only necessity made her harden her heart. And his repeated words helped her to do it. He wanted her, he kept saying; he needed her. And as far as he was concerned that was all there was to it. He wanted her to satisfy a masculine need too long dormant, while she, poor fool, was in love with him.

'No, Breid!' Pride gave her refusal greater weight, lent fluency to her excuses. 'It's nothing personal. I told you I like to move on. I just don't want to get involved— tied down with *any* man,' she emphasised. 'I'm not the person to give you what you want. I'm sorry.'

He lifted his head and looked at her. The grey-blue eyes were not angry now. Instead they held a touching uncertainty that smote her to her very core. Every fibre of Giana's being yearned over him. She wanted this man, wanted him with a physical intensity that was a gnawing pain inside her.

'I see,' he said stiffly. 'It seems I've made rather a fool of myself.' He straightened his back, his arms fell slackly at his side and he stepped away from her. 'I apologise.' And, as she stared at him, numbly trying to cope with her own anguish, 'Perhaps it would be best if we did terminate your employment. I'm only sorry,' and his voice was cold now, hatefully sarcastic, 'that it looks as if you have to put up with me for another twenty-four hours.'

CHAPTER SIX

How she got through the rest of that dreadful Sunday Giana hardly knew. By an unspoken agreement she and Breid avoided each other's company, an easy enough task in the vast old mill, meeting only for awkard silent meals. Dusk came and soon the darkness and they bade each other a stiff, formal goodnight.

For Giana it was most certainly not a good night. Most of it was spent in sleepless anguish until finally, just before dawn, she fell into an unrefreshing dream-beset slumber.

She woke, still weary and depressed, and when she looked out of her bedroom window she saw with mixed feelings that the flood waters had substantially receded; the pattern of dykes and fences was visible once more. A pale reluctant sun shone and gulls with their harsh, half-laughing cries drifted idly over the flat countryside. With a heart that ached, she realised there was nothing to prevent them leaving this lonely bird-haunted solitude which could have been so romantic a setting for love.

If only Breid had not spoken yesterday, she mourned as she showered and dressed. If only their enforced isolation had not precipitated those impassioned moments in each others' arms, she could have made some legitimate excuse to go back to London and set the wheels in motion for her divorce. Once she was no longer legally bound to Anthony, how gladly—with a clear conscience—she would have given herself to Breid

Winterton. He might not love her, yet. But, nurtured by physical completion, love might have grown. Now, instead, his male pride humiliated by her refusal, he obviously couldn't wait to be rid of her. A terrible sadness swamped her at the thought of what might have been. She didn't know how she was going to face the next few hours, the long, necessarily silent journey home. Polite conversation would be even worse, somehow. And then, at Foxdene Manor, the final parting. Her throat ached with tears that threatened, too, to fill her eyes. She forced them back as she went slowly downstairs.

'How soon can you be ready to leave?' Breid asked her abruptly as she entered the kitchen in search of coffee. Food would choke her, she knew. She noticed he had already eaten with no apparent ill effects. His expressionless face might not have been that of the man who had shown such deep emotions yesterday.

'We can go right away if you like,' she said quietly. She had packed her few possessions before coming downstairs.

'You don't want anything to eat?' Polite surprise only. He didn't give a damn. Tears rose to the surface again.

'No.' She avoided looking at him. Even on the simple monosyllable it was hard to keep her voice steady and he must have noticed the slight quiver.

'Giana?' He sounded suddenly uncertain, less formal. 'Is something wrong?' He made a half-step towards her and her insides quivered, responding as they always did to the masculine aura of him.

'What should be wrong?' she forced herself to say lightly. 'The floods have gone down. We can get away...' She had been going to say 'from this God-forsaken spot,' but already the old mill had come to mean something to her and she couldn't go on, couldn't keep up the pretence. Her voice broke and she pressed her knuckles hard against her mouth in a vain attempt to hold back a betraying sob.

'Giana . . .' The coldness had altogether gone from his voice; it was full of concern. 'There is something wrong. God, what a fool I am.' He ran one agitated hand through silvering blond hair. 'I know what it is. It's what happened yesterday, isn't it?' He sounded contrite now. 'You have a kind, compassionate, caring nature and I mistook your interest in my troubles for something more. What's more, unfairly, I took advantage of our situation here . . .'

'No, Breid, please don't.' Giana's innate fairness couldn't let him go on castigating himself. He wasn't any more to blame than she was. It must have seemed as if she was deliberately leading him on. But she'd wanted him, too, wanted him with a physical intensity that was still a persistent throbbing ache inside her. And she loved him so. She looked up and met his blue-grey eyes, her own drowning in the tears that refused to be held back. But through those tears her feelings for him glittered with an intensity that only a blind man could have missed. And Breid was far from blind.

And he knew. Suddenly he knew. It was there in his face, an expression of total comprehension, and he moved towards her, arms outstretched.

'What a fool I am!' He said again. 'What a crass, insensitive idiot you must think me. I'm not just rusty at making love, am I, but in the right words to go with it? I know now why you very properly turned me down flat.' His hands rested gently on her shoulders and he gave her a little rallying shake. 'Giana, dearest Giana, believe me, I may be a fool but I'm not an unprincipled swine, too. I wouldn't ask you to give yourself to me physically unless I'd fallen in love with you. And oh, Giana, I *do* love you, very very much.'

It took a second or two for his words to sink in. Her tear-drenched eyes widened in disbelief. Then, 'Breid! Oh, no!' It was an agonised cry. 'Please don't say any more, please don't.' For a moment her heart had leapt crazily, exultantly. But it wasn't fair to let him go on, to commit himself, at least not yet.

'But I *do* love you, Giana,' he reiterated. 'It's more than I'd ever hoped to know in this world again. Don't you understand? I'm not just asking you for physical satisfaction. I'm asking you to love me, in every sense of the word, and somehow I believe you do?' he questioned gently. 'That's why I was so stunned yesterday when you denied it. Please tell me I'm right.'

'I can't,' she almost sobbed. 'Please don't ask me, Breid. And please don't ask me why. There are reasons...'

'No good ones that I can think of.' His eyes shone triumphantly now. 'And you haven't denied that you love me, Giana.' His voice softened. 'Is it anything to do with Francesca? Because this was her home? Because you feel a certain delicacy about our making love here? I tell you most sincerely, Giana, Fran wouldn't have wanted me to be lonely for the rest of my life.'

'It isn't...' she began, but he went on inexorably.

'We talked about it once, Francesca and I, about one or the other of us dying. Half jokingly of course, the way people do about something they don't really think will happen to them. But all the same we meant what we said. You needn't be afraid of ghosts, Giana. I can't promise to forget Fran—she'll always have her own place in my heart—but *you* would have *your* place.' He cupped her chin, looked deeply into her eyes. 'I need your love, Giana and you do feel something for me, too, I'll swear you do. And in that case why shouldn't we...'

'No!' she cried frantically. She tried to pull free of him, but his clasp was too strong. 'Breid, you can't be certain yet that you're in love with me. You know nothing about me. We know so little about each other.'

'But you can't deny your feelings,' he insisted. 'They were there in your eyes just now. Your body trembles with wanting when I touch you. Giana, I'm alone, you're alone.' And, as her head drooped, her hair swinging forward to disguise the longing his words aroused, 'Why, I believe you're just shy.' His voice was heart-tuggingly tender. 'And perhaps I've spoken too soon?'

'Yes,' she seized eagerly on this, but she nodded without looking up at him. She dared not.

'I understand,' he went on reassuringly, 'why you feel you don't really know me. Though I'm sure I know enough about you to know that I love you. But I should have waited a little longer, given you more time. I'm prepared to wait, Giana,' he said to her downbent head. 'I promise I won't touch you again in any intimate way until you give me the word, if you'll only give me some hope for the future. I'm not just asking for your love, my darling. I want to marry you and as soon as possible. I want you so much. Next month, next week even, wouldn't be too soon for me.'

'That's impossible!' Now her head did jerk up and the cry was torn from her trembling lips.

'Why is it impossible for you to marry me?' He sounded almost angry again.

'I didn't mean that,' she stopped short. She already knew what she meant to do. She knew that whatever happened when Anthony came back to her, there was no way she could go on living with him as his wife, living a lie. She respected her parents' opinions, their right to them, but she was twenty-four now, old enough to make her own decisions about what was right and what was wrong. Even before Breid's declaration she'd already decided she was going to ask Anthony for a divorce.

And in that case would it be so wrong to promise to marry Breid, to let him make love to her, as they both wanted, here, now? After all, no one, certainly not Anthony, would be hurt by it. What they did here, on their own, in the privacy and isolation of The Retreat, was their business.

Yet old mores and disciplines were hard to break. And then, too, Giana was frightened. Numbly she acknowledged the reason. If she admitted her love for Breid, gave him the promise he demanded and let him make love to her, she would have to tell him they couldn't be married at once. He would want to know why and she would have to tell him she was already married. Breid knew her as Giana Spencer. She could let him think that was her husband's name, but how long would the deception last? Giana was nothing if not realistic; there was no way a secret like that could be kept for ever. She dreaded Breid's reaction when he discovered she was married to his *bête noir*, Anthony Leyburn. Eventually she would have to tell him, but she wanted to choose her own moment. She seized upon the promise he had made of patience.

'I can't give you an answer immediately,' she told him flatly, her emotions almost under control now. 'You were right, I do need more time. It's all happened too quickly, too suddenly.'

'But you're not turning me down altogether!' He was jubilant now, hugging her to him, and Giana was hard put to it not to fling her arms about him and tell him she wanted this delay as little as he. He drew away a fraction and scrutinised her flushed troubled face. 'We'll go back to Dinas Mead and start getting to know each other. I'm going to court you properly, Giana.'

He looked and sounded as if he might be about to begin the process right now, and, gently but firmly, Giana freed herself. She wasn't sure her willpower could withstand another emotional onslaught.

'Are *you* ready to leave?' she asked him and heard him sigh.

'Yes, we'll go now. But we'll be back again some day,' he averred, 'together.'

Breid's ankle was still sore but he insisted it was recovered enough for him to be able to drive. The Rolls-Royce slipped and slid across the muddy sea the landscape had become, but gallantly the elderly vehicle gained their first objective, the Fisherman's Return. Here Breid briefly explained their non-appearance, but the landlord refused his offer to settle their account.

'It's just nice to see you back in these parts, Mr Winterton, sir. I hopes as how we'll be seeing more of you in future—and the lady, perhaps?' The elderly man's eyes assessed Giana and obviously approved what they saw.

'I hope so, too, Fred.' The gaze Breid turned on her was as partial and vastly more, making Giana tremble with the intensity of her feelings for him.

While they were at the inn, Breid telephoned ahead to warn his housekeeper of their imminent return.

'Don't think I'm ungrateful or critical,' he told Giana. 'You made the best you could of what was available, but I'm certainly looking forward to getting back to Mary Pimblett's home cooking.'

With the cessation of the rain, the Norfolk countryside had taken on a more cheerful aspect and Giana found her spirits rising proportionately. A few more weeks, a few months of Breid's promised tolerance, and she would be free to express her love for him. He would be justifiably annoyed at first when he learned the whole truth about her and about the reason for her appearance in his life, but if *he* loved *her* as much as he said he did, he would understand the necessity for and forgive her deception.

The weather improved as they drove south and by the time they reached the old manor house the day was almost springlike. Crossing the threshold of Foxdene once more was like coming home. It would be her home some day, Giana promised herself as she looked around the timbered hall with its polished floors and twinkling brasses. The journey back had been a pleasant one with Breid in a sunny talkative mood that revealed to her something of the private man he had kept so deeply hidden.

Mrs Pimblett in a voluminous flowered overall gave them a warm welcome.

'I'm right glad to see you,' she told Breid. 'Folks have been pestering with messages for you. Publishers, agents. One gentleman phoned yesterday and I told him I didn't know when you'd be back. He called again this morning, just after you spoke to me. He says he has to see you, urgent. He'll be here mid-afternoon. It's my day for shopping, so will you listen out and let him in?'

'Damn,' Breid said with feeling after Mrs Pimblett had bustled away to check on the progress of lunch. 'I was hoping we'd have the place to ourselves this afternoon.' He put down the suitcases he had carried in from the car and took Giana in his arms, the contact weakening her limbs. 'But there's always this evening—and tonight. Oh, Giana,' he murmured huskily, 'I'm going to enjoy teaching you to love me.'

At his suggestive tone, quivering warmth erupted in the lower half of her body. It was tempting to nestle close to him, to return his embrace. He was an intensely sexual man. Whenever he was close to her she seemed unable to function properly.

'I . . .' She ran her tongue across lips grown dry with nerves, for he wasn't going to like what she had to say. 'I won't be here this evening.'

'Not here?' His voice was sharp with surprised affront. 'What do you mean?' It deepened to certainty. 'Of course you'll be here.'

'No.' She tried to move out of the circle of his arms but his hold tightened. 'I have to go back to London for a few days.'

'That's the first I've heard of it. For God's sake, why? What's so important that you have to go away just when we've agreed we're really going to spend some time discovering each other?'

'It *is* important, very important,' Giana insisted, 'and I can't discuss it right now. It…it's too personal. Maybe when I come back . . .'

'But why tonight? Surely another few hours won't make any difference. Leave it until tomorrow,' he urged, 'and I'll drive you up to town myself.' Drily, 'That way I can make sure you *do* come back.'

'No!' Distractedly she shook her head, the long fair hair fanning from side to side. 'This is something I have to do alone. And I promise you I will come back.' She sought for words that would convince him. 'I . . . I *want* to come back to you, Breid. Please believe that.'

'Then you do already care a little?' His grasp slackened but he eased her closer. He bent his head and his mouth touched the side of her neck, tracing the long slender lines of it. 'I believe you, Giana,' he murmured against the sensitive flesh just behind her ear. 'Part of loving is trust. Just don't be away from me too long, hmm?' His fingers slid into her hair, shaping her head, stroking the nape of her neck whilst his mouth found hers. His lips lingered, caressing, tasting her with a sensual languor as seductive as his more fervent kisses had been.

Although he was gentle, his body was urgent against her so that she was aware of the intensity of his desire, and she shuddered violently, wanting to know his possession now, immediately. As though it were no longer under her control her hand lifted to touch his face, her palm caressing the lean planes, the angular bone structure.

'Oh, Giana, can't it wait until tomorrow, whatever it is?' he breathed urgently against her lips and before she could reply his hands moved swiftly over her body in a comprehensive caress awakening in her a reciprocal hunger. It seemed incredible that in such a short acquaintance they could have aroused in each other such violent feelings.

'Leave it until tomorrow, Giana,' he urged again. 'Stay with me tonight.'

Almost she agreed. But she knew what would happen if she stayed. He would make love to her. And with each hour that passed her resistance to him would weaken. At the mental image of those hours and how they would be spent shudders of sensation gripped her body.

'I have to go today,' she told him with a greater firmness than she felt, and she was relieved when Mary Pimblett emerged from the kitchen with the announcement that lunch was ready. The housekeeper seemed not a whit perturbed at finding her employer holding his secretary in his arms. In fact, Giana thought she detected a gleam of approval in Mary's faded eyes.

'Well, at least you're having something to eat before you leave,' Breid insisted. 'You had no breakfast.'

'All right,' Giana agreed, albeit reluctantly. Some instinct of self-preservation told her she ought to go now, this minute, perhaps because she feared he might go on trying to persuade her otherwise. It was a decision she would shortly regret.

'How long will you be away?' Breid asked as they sat on either side of the table and Mary Pimblett served generous helpings of a warming beef stew.

'I don't know,' Giana confessed. It wouldn't take long to instruct a solicitor, but she felt she must see Anthony and tell him face to face what she planned. Surely by now someone must know where she could contact him.

'You must have some idea, surely?' he pressed. 'One day? Two?'

'It might be longer than that. I honestly don't know. I'll telephone you when I do.' Giana could see he was wishing he could force some definite answer from her, but as the housekeeper took her meals with them further pressure was impossible.

Breid had just asked for coffee and Mary Pimblett
was in the kitchen preparing it when the front doorbell
rang.

'I'll go, Mary,' Breid called.

Giana hoped the visitor would keep him occupied for
some time. It would make her leavetaking easier if there
were no opportunity for protracted farewells.

'Make that coffee for four, Mary,' she heard Breid
call from the hallway. Then, to the unseen arrival, 'This
way. I hope you don't mind us still being at the table?
Have you eaten?'

The caller made some assent, followed Breid into the
dining-room, then stopped short.

'Good God!' he exclaimed, then he withdrew swiftly
into the hall and in an urgent voice demanded of Breid
if there were somewhere else they could talk.

Giana had no need to wonder why. The astrakhan-
collared coat and hat, the jaunty bowtie were all too
familiar. It was the watcher, Mr Ellis of Ellis and Palmer.
Anthony's shadow. And she had no doubt that he knew
who she was. As a bewildered Breid ushered the inquiry
agent into his office, she got up from the table and
tiptoed into the hall. Her overnight suitcase was still
where Breid had set it down but her car keys were in her
bedroom. Stealthily she made for the stairs. With her
foot on the bottom step there came an interruption.

'The coffee's made, Miss Spencer.' Mary Pimblett
stood in the hall bearing a loaded tray and common
courtesy dictated that Giana return and open the dining-
room door for her.

'Don't pour one for me, Mrs Pimblett,' she said in a
low unsteady voice which drew a curious glance from
the older woman. 'I find I haven't time for it after all.
I've got a long drive ahead of me.' Not waiting for pro-

tests or questions, she fled, and this time successfully gained her bedroom. She snatched up her handbag and rummaged feverishly to make sure her keys were in it. At the reassuring rattle she turned on her heel, intending to make for the door which she'd left open behind her. It was closed. And against it leant a furiously angry Breid Winterton. His face was that of a total stranger—a stranger she feared.

'Surely you weren't thinking of leaving without saying goodbye—*Mrs Leyburn*?' The ice in his voice, she thought numbly, would have frozen a whole consignment of perishable food.

Giana's still open handbag slipped from her nerveless fingers, its contents distributing themselves widespread over the thick pile carpet. Twice she opened her mouth to speak and failed. The third time she managed a dry croaking sound.

'Breid, please, let me explain.'

'Oh, yes! And what an explanation that would be!' He was bitingly sarcastic. 'I've no doubt your fertile imagination could conjure up even more fantastic lies than those you've already told me, but it's not going to get the chance.' He moved away from the door and advanced towards her, infinitely menacing, looking taller than ever as he bent his silver-blond head to avoid the low oak beams that supported the ceiling. 'How you must have been laughing up your sleeve, *Mrs Leyburn*, at my gullibility.'

'Oh, no, Breid,' she pleaded. 'I . . .'

'Oh, yes, Mrs Leyburn.' He was standing over her now and vaguely on the periphery of her mind she heard the case of a lipstick crack beneath his feet. He took her upper arms in a punishing grip, steely fingers biting into her flesh even through the thickness of her sweater. 'Your unscrupulous husband knew *he* didn't stand a cat in hell's chance of setting foot over my threshold again, didn't he? So he sent you to do his dirty work, while he seduced my daughter. The daughter you've been pretending to help me find.'

'No,' she protested.

'Oh, yes. You knew all about those lying love letters. "Love!" It was all a pretence and *you* knew what was going on. You know what that makes you, don't you?'

'It wasn't *like* that!' a horrified Giana exclaimed. 'If you'd only let me...' But he went on inexorably, his fingers biting deeper still.

'Only it was me that nearly got seduced, wasn't it? What were you hoping to make out of that, the pair of you? My God!' he said savagely, 'When I think of the fatuous things I've said to you in the last few days. How did you manage to keep a straight face? I suppose you've been making notes.'

'Breid!' His name came out on a sob. 'Stop it, please.'

'What sort of story was he after this time?' He gave her an ungentle shake, making her sag against him like a rag doll. 'Were you supposed to get me into bed so that some *paparazzi* could bob up and take compromising photographs? Are you so lost to all sense of decency that you let your husband use you in that way?'

'If that's what you think,' she almost shouted at him, incensed, 'why did I refuse to...?'

'Maybe the timing wasn't right?' he suggested sarcastically. 'Perhaps you'd arranged a different rendezvous with your photographer? Poor Giana,' he jeered. 'How alarmed you must have been when you thought you might be forced to use your so beautiful body to no avail. Or wouldn't you have objected to a repeat performance for the sake of a good story?'

'You've got it all wrong.' Unheeded tears lay damply on her cheeks. 'I was going to tell you...'

'And where's my daughter, damn you?' He shook her again. 'Where's that husband of yours hiding her? Is he holding her to ransom or something? Is it money he's after?'

'I don't know where she is,' Giana sobbed. 'I didn't know anything about Anthony's involvement with your daughter until you told me. Those letters were a shock to me. I...'

'Liar!' he said savagely. 'My God, to think such beauty could mask such depravity.' Breid's eyes narrowed as he scrutinised her pale face. 'And to think I... Of course,' he went on softly, 'Leyburn had met Francesca. He couldn't fail to recognise the likeness. The unscrupulous swine! He knew my Achilles' heel, didn't he? He made use of your resemblance to my wife.' He fell into a brooding silence but at least it gave Giana a chance to speak.

'Oh, Breid, please, please believe me. It wasn't like that. Anthony doesn't know where I am any more than I know where he is. I would have told you about him before we... And I would never do anything to hurt you. I...I love you.' As she said it she knew it was a futile effort. But she had to tell him. It would be her last, her only opportunity to do so.

'You love me!' The words held a wealth of scorn, of bitterness. 'That's rich!'

Giana felt as though his iron-hard fingers must soon break her arms in two.

'Breid, please,' she begged. 'You're hurting me.'

'Not half as much as I'm going to hurt you before you leave here. I can't lay hands on Leyburn, but by God I'm going to lay hands on his wife.'

'You . . . you wouldn't. Breid, I keep telling you, I'm not working with Anthony. You said love included trust, you said you loved me.' Giana wasn't afraid so much of physical violence as of the irrevocable destruction it would bring to their relationship.

'Perhaps I lied, too!' he told her harshly. 'Perhaps I told you that because I knew it was the only way I could get what I wanted.'

'No,' Giana denied. 'You're not like that. I *know* you're not.'

'But you said yourself you know nothing about me.' Bitterly, 'I certainly knew less than I thought I did about you.'

'And you still don't know me,' she urged. 'Everything you've said about me just now is totally wrong. Please, Breid, don't do something you'll regret.'

'Oh, I don't think I shall regret it,' he said silkily and there was a disturbing glint in his eyes. He jerked her suddenly against him. His hips jutted painfully against her own. His body moved against her making her aware that he was aroused. He was going to kiss her, she realised in shocked disbelief. But not out of love or even desire. He was angry, and he was going to relieve all that anger in an assault upon her.

As she tried to make one last plea for mercy, for understanding, his mouth covered hers. His kiss was hard and aggressive, taking advantage of her parted lips to thrust savagely with his tongue.

The probing intimacy made her pulses quiver frantically and in spite of everything she could not stop herself responding to him. She moaned softly as his tongue explored the inner softness of her mouth, the kiss going on and on, weakening her to the point of collapse so that hands which should have been pushing him away clung for support to the thick wool of his sweater. She could feel and hear the heavy beat of his heart as he leaned back, lifting her, pulling her against the throbbing bulk of his desire. Erotic pleasure swamped her as his hand slid beneath her sweater and sought the bur- geoning fullness of her silk-covered breasts, her nipples tightening and thrusting to his touch.

A shudder of physical need convulsed her and delib- erately he let her slide down the whole length of his hardened body, eased her backwards until she felt the edge of the bed against her legs. His hips moved rhythmically against hers as his impatient hand made short work of the fastening of her bra. Further and further her back arched until, their equilibrium totally lost, together they overbalanced. Giana fell on to the bed, Breid's heavy weight almost crushing the breath from her.

She wanted to explore his body as he was exploring hers, to convince him somehow of her love. Beneath the rough woollen sweater his skin was bare, satin-smooth, dewed with a light perspiration. She ran her fingers over the taut muscles, found the little depression where the base of his spine met the hollow of his buttocks, and she heard him groan as her fingers delved into the warm silken soft groove.

He was becoming irritated with the clothes that sep- arated them from closer intimacies. He pushed up her sweater so that he could see the breasts he had exposed and she felt the erotic play of his mouth around the tense excited nipples.

'I want you,' he muttered. 'I want to be closer to you, to be inside you. Damn it, how can I still want you, in spite of everything?'

'Because you know in your heart what you've said about me isn't true,' she told him imploringly.

It was a shock when he laughed savagely.

'In my heart! No! Oh, I want you in my bed, Giana, but forget sentiment. My heart has nothing to do with it. This is sex, Giana, pure and simple. But it will do. A starving man will make do with a crust.' He bent his head towards her breasts again but this time she managed to hold him off.

'And that's all it ever has been, sex,' she accused. 'You told me you didn't want me just because I reminded you of Francesca. But that's what it was. All you wanted me for was to relieve the frustrations of loving a dead woman.'

He went very still. Then he thrust himself upright and stood above her, his legs straddling hers, preventing her from moving even if she could have found the strength to do so. His hands were clenched and for a moment Giana actually believed he would strike her. But when he spoke his words were more painful than any blow.

'Don't you dare to compare yourself with Francesca, just because some unfortunate freak of nature has given you her likeness. You're not fit to mention her name. There's only one thing in this whole wretched business that I'm glad of. Thank God I *didn't* take you to bed under Francesca's roof.'

'You didn't have the chance!' she snapped. Out of her pain her own temper rose to protect her pride. But, she recognised suddenly, Breid didn't want to fight any more.

He had stepped back from the bed and his expression was cold and unutterably weary.

'Get up, Mrs Leyburn. Take your belongings and get out of my house. I find the sight of you utterly sickening.'

CHAPTER SEVEN

AN OBSCENE smear like blood stained the carpet where the crushed lipstick had been ground into the apricot pile. Huddled on the bedroom floor, Giana gathered up the scattered contents of her handbag. Her hand shook and her tear-filled eyes saw refracted, glimmering images of her possessions.

Aware of Breid's cold, hostile stare following her every move, she cleared drawers, wardrobes and dressing-table, the items flung at random into her second case. She had a struggle to close it but Breid made no move to help her.

It seemed strange and coldly final to leave without some parting word, but what was there either of them could say?

She was thankful when he didn't follow her downstairs.

The study door was ajar. As she paused to pick up her overnight bag, Giana noticed that the inquiry agent hadn't left. He was sitting bolt upright on a hard chair, feet planted neatly together. He saw her, too.

'Mrs Leyburn, a word, if you please.'

As he rose to his feet, Giana fled. She didn't want to talk to him or to anyone. Somehow, though she now carried two suitcases, she negotiated the heavy front door and almost ran to her car.

She flung her luggage on to the back seat and prayed the vehicle would start. She hadn't used it since she came to Dinas Mead.

The engine fired first time. Wheels spinning on the loose, still rain-wet gravel of the drive, Giana left Foxdene Manor.

It was a wonder, she thought afterwards, that she'd made the journey to London without any mishap. She must have driven on 'automatic pilot' most of the way because her brain had spiralled in frantic circles, going over and over the events of the past hours, culminating in Breid's contemptuous dismissal of her. Round and round again her thoughts went, always covering the same territory, each repetition worse than the last.

She thanked heaven she had left the flat's central heating on, for she was tired, dispirited and very cold when she reached Godolphin Buildings and garaged the car. Even so the apartment had an emptiness, an atmosphere that increased her inner chill. It was loneliness. Giana had never felt more alone in the whole of her life.

For extra warmth she lit the gasfire, switched on every light for an illusion of cheer, put on the radio for company. Then she was at a loss for further occupation, yet she couldn't sit still. It was only ten o'clock, not too late to telephone friends or family. But she didn't feel like social chatter. And if she spoke to either of her parents they would know without her telling them that something was wrong.

In the end she set herself the task of cleaning the flat, which showed signs of its two-week neglect.

But when, physically exhausted, she went to bed, her mind was still frantically active. If only she'd never gone to Dinas Mead. If only she'd never met Breid Winterton. And, more importantly, if only she hadn't been fool enough to fall in love with him. Before she'd met Breid she'd been reasonably content, or at least resigned to her lot. Now she was prey to a destroying mental and physical torture and to unattainable dreams.

She'd made up her mind to cut short her holiday and return to work next day, and had just fallen into an uneasy doze, when the bedside telephone rang. Startled, disoriented, she knocked the instrument flying and had to grope on the floor for it. When finally, breathlessly, she gave her number, she recognised Fay Pratt's agitated voice.

'Giana? Whatever's happening there?'

'Nothing. I'm OK. I just knocked the phone over.'

'Oh, Giana,' Fay went on, 'I've been so worried. I've been ringing the flat for the past two days. I didn't know where else to try. You promised to keep in touch.' It was only two days since Giana had last telephoned Fay.

'Not that often,' she protested. 'Anyway I couldn't get to a phone yesterday and I've been travelling all day today.'

'Well thank God you're home now. I was afraid you might have done something . . . something silly.'

She had, reflected Giana wryly, very silly. But she wasn't going to tell Fay about that.

'Giana? Are you still there? Are you all right?'

'Yes, of course I'm all right. Why shouldn't I be?' But she'd never felt at a lower ebb and Giana wondered if perhaps Fay Pratt possessed some psychic faculty that had made her telephone tonight.

'Well I thought . . . you must have heard by now? The police . . .'

'The police! Heard what?' Immediately Giana's thoughts were of Breid. Something had happened to him. Then she relaxed. Fay had been trying to contact her for two days. Breid had been all right only a few hours ago.

'Heard what?' she repeated.

'Oh, dear!' Fay wailed. She sounded quite unlike the calm, efficient woman Giana knew. 'So you don't know.'

'Know what, for goodness sake?'

But Fay had pulled herself together.

'I'm coming round. I won't be long. Stay right where you are.' The line went dead.

Ten minutes later a taxi deposited Fay Pratt at Godolphin Buildings, by which time a yawning Giana had dressed and put the kettle on, a task that Fay's agitated manner seemed to warrant. It must be a disaster of some proportion to bring the older woman out at midnight. Oddly enough, Giana did not connect the event with herself but assumed Fay had troubles of some kind. Accustomed to being the recipient of other people's confidences, it didn't even occur to Giana to wonder why Fay should turn to her, when the other woman had close friends of her own age and social circle.

'Fay, come in. I've made some tea, or would you rather have coffee?'

'Haven't you got anything stronger?'

'I don't think so.' Giana was puzzled. She didn't drink spirits and she didn't believe Fay did either. 'Anthony only drinks other people's whisky,' she explained drily. As she preceded her visitor into the sitting-room, Giana thought Fay gave her a strange glance. 'Sit down,' Giana invited.

'You'd better sit down, too,' Fay urged. Then, 'Giana, I don't know any way of breaking this gently, but…I've got news of Anthony.'

'Oh?' Giana was almost uninterested. A few hours ago she would have been glad, if not exactly looking forward to confronting her husband, so she could tell him she wanted a divorce. Now it didn't really seem to matter. Whether she were divorced or not, Breid wouldn't want anything more to do with her.

'Giana, you must try and be brave. Do you remember, about two weeks ago, a charter flight that crashed into the sea?' and, as Giana nodded, 'Giana, dear, Anthony was on that flight.' Giana stared at her uncomprehendingly. 'A lot of…of people weren't found right away. Then, two days ago, they found…Anthony.'

'Anthony!' Giana repeated, then, as the sense of Fay's words began to penetrate. 'You don't mean…you mean Anthony's…*dead*?'

'Yes. Oh, dear, please don't… You're hysterical.' For Giana had begun to laugh, a high, mirthless, dreadful laugh, unnaturally shrill. Fay put her arm around Giana's shoulders. 'Come on now, dear, I know it's the shock, but you really mustn't take on like that.'

A shock! Yes, it was. Reaction set in and Giana began to cry, great shuddering sobs that racked her whole body.

'That's it, dear,' Fay sounded relieved. 'That's better. You have a good cry. I know I'd be just the same if anything happened to my Simon.'

And she *had* been crying for Anthony, Giana thought soberly hours later when the older woman had left. Fay had not gone without first insisting that she ought to stay the night, or at least take Giana home with her.

She'd cried for Anthony because he had been her husband and she had loved him once, and it was a tragedy that anyone should die. But she knew she was crying for herself, too, for Breid, for the whole hopeless useless mess life seemed to have become.

There was no point in going back to bed. She would have to visit the local police station first thing in the morning. The police had also been trying to contact her.

'Mrs Leyburn?' The policewoman was young and concerned. 'I'm sorry to have to ask you this, but were you still living with Mr Leyburn?'

'Yes, that is . . .'

'You weren't divorced or separated?' And, as Giana stared at her, 'You see, Mrs Leyburn, the aeroplane passenger list showed a Mr and Mrs Leyburn travelling together. But so far no other body has been recovered. We wondered if you'd intended to travel, then changed your mind at the last moment?'

'No,' Giana said huskily. 'I wasn't planning to travel with my husband. He . . .'

'Then the other Mrs Leyburn?' The young policewoman was being diplomatic. 'Was it your mother-in-law, perhaps?'

'No,' Giana said flatly. 'My husband's mother died a long time ago. It's all right,' she told the young officer. 'You don't have to be tactful. I know he was seeing someone else. I . . .' Then with full force it struck her. 'You said no other body had been recovered? That means she . . . she's dead, too?'

Tina dead, too. Oh, God, what was this going to do to Breid after all the other tragedies in his life?

'It seems very likely. Did you know this other woman, Mrs Leyburn? Can you tell us her name? We shall have to contact her relatives.'

'Oh, no!' Giana cried, then, taking a grip of herself. 'I mean no, I don't know who she is...was.' It was another lie to add to her already overburdened conscience, a serious lie this time, too. This time she was obstructing the police in the execution of their duties. But she couldn't let Breid hear news like this from an impersonal stranger. He had no one now, no one to turn to in his grief.

He might round on her, abuse her, turn her from his door again. But even though he might not let her comfort him, she *had* to be the one to break the news to him about Tina. That was the very least she could do for him.

'I see.' It didn't sound as if the young policewoman altogether believed her. 'Well, in that case...'

'Will I...will I have to identify my husband...my husband's body?' Giana had seen dead people in the course of her work but had never had such intimate contact before with the deceased.

'No. Mr Pratt, your husband's employer, kindly offered to spare you that task. Have you someone to take care of funeral arrangements for you?'

'Yes, my father. He's a vicar,' Giana said absently, her thoughts still with Breid. She rose to leave. 'Will...will they go on looking for...for the other body?'

'For a while, I imagine. But you don't need to worry yourself about that, Mrs Leyburn,' the policewoman said as she ushered Giana from the interview room.

The next few days passed in a grey fog. Giana's first instinct had been to rush down to Dinas Mead, but that was impossible. In any case she couldn't leave town until after Anthony's funeral. But nor could she go straight to Breid so soon after hearing of her husband's death. No matter that Anthony had been deceiving her all these months, nor that he'd actually died deceiving her. No matter that their marriage would soon have ended anyway. The very fact of his death demanded her respect.

The Reverend and Mrs Spencer came up to London immediately they heard the news. There were Anthony's brothers and sisters to be contacted, and after the funeral Giana's mother insisted she would stay in town for a few days. She was concerned at her daughter's wan looks and what she saw as unnatural control. There was not point in grieving her parents by telling them the full facts behind the disaster.

On the Saturday following the funeral Mrs Spencer left reluctantly for home.

'I can't leave your father to cope with Sunday all on his own.' She'd been unable to persuade Giana to accompany her.

And the next afternoon Giana herself set out on the familiar journey into Kent.

It was almost April now and out of the recent rains spring had risen, full-grown and lusty, many-coloured. It was almost possible to forget the sorry nature of her errand, the apprehension she felt about confronting Breid again. In the spring sunlight even the motorway with its crop of Sunday afternoon motorists was pleasant. And how enjoyable it was to leave the main roads and drive through the steep winding tree-lined lanes, through small picturesque hamlets with their evocative names, Ivy Hatch and Cream Crox, to pass old stone houses with hundreds of years' history in their walls.

There was a silken sheen to the pale edges of the young beech leaves, a silvery shimmer to the shadowy boles of the trees.

Spring, a time of new beginnings, Giana thought, the resurrection of life and of hope. Even a flat tyre did not entirely deflate her mood of optimism as she rehearsed what she would say to Breid.

First, gently, she would break the news about Tina. Then she would tell him of Anthony's death. Intensely practical, Giana wasn't normally given to daydreaming, but today as she drove on she allowed herself to imagine Breid, softened by his bereavement, mellowing towards her enough to allow her to explain how and why she'd first come to Dinas Mead. Then, still dreaming, she envisaged a tender scene in which, all their differences reconciled, they would affirm their love for each other.

It was all so beautiful, she could almost imagine it had really happened, and it was with a sense of shock that she came back to cold reality, realised she was almost at her destination and that her bright dreams were all still to be accomplished, might never be realised.

It was late afternoon when she stopped in Dinas Mead at the Cock and Bull. She'd hoped to be able to book one of their two guest-rooms and deposit her overnight bag. Daydreaming was gone. She was back to reality and reality told her it wasn't likely she'd be invited to spend the night at Foxdene. It was more conceivable that after the confrontation with Breid she wouldn't feel up to driving straight back to London. She was unlucky, both of the inn's guestrooms were taken, but the landlord was obliging. He telephoned the next village, some ten miles further on beyond Dinas Mead; the landlady of the George and Dragon, he told Giana, would be happy to accommodate her.

In the car once more she sat for a few moments, gripping the steering-wheel, nerving herself to take the last lap of her journey, past the church and up the steep lane to the gates of Foxdene Manor. Not wanting to give notice of her arrival, she parked her car just inside the gates and walked up the winding gravel drive.

It was like her first arrival all over again, as if there had been a time-slip. On the doorstep of the old, timbered manor house, she rang the bell, two, three times.

Slowly she walked around the side of the building, to the rear where the conservatory door again yielded to her touch. Some of the lush tropical plants bore flower buds, she noticed. Her emotions running high, senses attuned, details of her surroundings stood out in unusually sharp detail.

The office was just as she remembered, only this time no tall man sat in the leather swivel chair. Giana hesitated to go any further. And yet if she were to see Breid she must.

There was no one in the kitchen. Of course, it was Mary Pimblett's day for shopping. There was no one in the dining-room. Breid didn't lunch at home, but he hadn't been at the Cock and Bull.

Giana had her hand on the drawing-room door when it opened abruptly.

'Good lord! What are *you* doing here?'

It wasn't Breid who faced her but a tall, slender girl of about her own height. Much younger though, dark-haired and extremely lovely. Her expression was hostile. She stood with the help of crutches.

'Tina!' Giana gasped, for she had recognised Breid's daughter immediately. 'You're safe, you're alive!' Weakly, 'Oh, thank God!'

'What have *you* got to be so pleased about?' the other demanded. 'Shouldn't you be wishing me dead?' She was belligerent but she was also very young, very apprehensive and on the defensive.

'I couldn't wish that on my worst enemy,' Giana said soberly. 'We're only given one life.'

'And I'm *not* your worst enemy, Mrs Leyburn?' The dark girl's voice was full of disbelief. She wheeled on her crutches and made her way back to the chair where she'd obviously been sitting before Giana's arrival. The area around it was carelessly littered with glossy magazines.

Giana ignored the remark. It was pointless to rake over the dead ashes of the past. Tina Winterton hadn't offered her a seat, but she took one anyway. She needed to sit down.

'You escaped from the plane crash!'

'Obviously!' Tina Winterton was still edgy. Her young face was mutinous but her eyes were wary.

'But how?'

'God knows!' She shrugged. 'I suppose someone must have dragged me out of the wreckage. I don't remember.'

'And how long have you been here?'

'Two or three days.' The young shoulders drooped. 'My father insisted. Talk about Gloomsville. I can't wait to get back to London.'

'How long has Breid . . .?' Giana flushed and amended, 'How long has your father known you were safe?'

'About a week. Since I got my memory back. Before that I had amnesia. They told me I'd had a crack on the head. For a while I had no idea who I was or what I was doing on that wretched plane. Mrs Leyburn...' She hesitated, then, 'How's Tony? Was he hurt?'

'Anthony wasn't as lucky as you,' Giana told her. 'He's dead.'

'Oh!' Tina obviously hadn't expected anything like that. She paled and for a moment her lips quivered. Then, defiantly, 'I suppose you blame me for that?'

'No,' Giana told her quietly. 'Anthony was old enough to make his own mistakes.'

The younger girl looked at her curiously.

'You don't sound like a devastated widow. But I suppose if your marriage had been a happy one Tony wouldn't have been playing the field.'

'You don't seem particularly grieved yourself,' Giana was stung to retort.

'I'm sorry he's dead, of course. He was fun to be with. He knew all the interesting people and he took me to some fabulous places. We were on our way to Paris when...'

'Is that all?' Giana exclaimed. 'Surely, if you were in love with him...'

'In love?' The younger girl shrugged. 'I wasn't. Not really. Oh, I was fond of him. And I felt sorry for him in a way. He wasn't as thick-skinned as he made out. He had a real chip on his shoulder, didn't he, about having been born in a slum? He did get a bit intense sometimes. But heavens above, he was almost old enough to be my father.'

'And he was married!' Giana was tart. 'Didn't that worry you at all?'

'Not really.' Tina was defiant again. 'If women can't hang on to their husbands, that's their look out. Besides, I don't believe in marriage.' She gave a toss of her dark head. 'It's old hat. Catch me getting married!'

Giana was at a loss for words. She could only stare at the younger girl and shake her head.

'Why have you come down here?' Tina asked curiously. 'Not to tell me about Tony, surely?'

'I didn't know you'd be here,' Giana reminded her. 'Actually I came down here to tell your father you were missing. I believed...'

'Thanks for the thought,' Tina said flippantly, 'but as you see it wasn't necessary. How is it you know my father?'

'I worked for him for...for a short while.'

'But Tony said you were a nurse...a starchy do-gooder he called you.' Tina clapped a hand over her mouth. 'I suppose I shouldn't have told you that.' But she didn't sound genuinely penitent.

'It's nothing new,' Giana said drily. 'He said it to my face often enough. I am a nurse, but I took a temporary job as your father's secretary because I wanted to know why he was having my husband followed.'

'He was?' Indignantly, 'The crafty old devil!' Then, curiously, 'He's never mentioned you. Did he know who you were?'

'Not at first.' Giana's face and voice were expressive.

'That sounds as if he found out. I bet he was bloody furious.' That was putting it mildly, Giana thought. 'Dad's not here, by the way,' Tina added.

It hadn't occurred to Giana that Breid might not be at Dinas Mead. When she'd thought of him, as she had done constantly in the past few days, she had imagined him at Foxdene Manor, following his usual routine. And like a fool she hadn't thought to make enquiries at the town house. She could have saved herself a journey which had turned out to be totally unnecessary. 'Do you know where he is?' she asked dully.

'Haven't a clue. Mrs P might know if she were here. I wish I wasn't here either. Once I get rid of these,' she indicated the crutches, 'Dinas Mead won't see me for dust.'

Giana rose to leave. There was no reason for her to stay, no excuse to see Breid just one more time.

'Mrs Leyburn?'

Giana turned in the doorway to look at Tina Winterton. The girl looked suddenly very vulnerable. 'I...I am sorry about Tony. And...and I'm sorry he was deceiving you. You're not a bit like I expected. Tony said...' Her voice trailed away. 'Oh, well, anyway, I'm sorry.'

Giana nodded curtly. She knew Tina could have played only a small part in Anthony's defection. She couldn't blame a young, inexperienced girl for falling for his facile charm; she'd done more or less the same thing herself. And in a way Giana blamed herself far more for their drifting apart. Of late, heavily involved with her work and other people's problems, she had made no attempt to counter the disenchantment she'd felt with her marriage. She was ashamed that it had taken a young girl like Tina to recognise Anthony's perennial problem, the basic inferiority that lay beneath the brash, hard-boiled image of the professional journalist.

'Mrs Leyburn!' Again Tina's voice halted her in the doorway. Looking at the girl Giana discerned an air of pathos. 'Do you have to go yet?' the girl pleaded. 'It's as quiet as the grave here. I'm bored out of my skull. Dad's away, Mrs P's been out for hours...' There was a distinct quiver to her lips as she added, 'and...and my leg aches abominably.'

A couple of hours later, after she'd persuaded Tina to go to bed, Giana was washing up in the manor's modernised kitchen. The last thing she'd expected, she mused, was to find herself feeling sorry for Tina Winterton. But she did. She also found herself remembering that Tina had been at a very awkward age when her mother had died. The girl was a strange mixture, half-child, half-adult, aggressive one moment, pathetic and oddly appealing the next. No wonder she'd made Anthony feel strong.

At Tina's plea Giana had turned back into the room.

'What would you like me to do?' she had asked gently. 'Stay and talk to you for a while? Or are you hungry? Shall I make you something to eat? It can't be easy to prepare food when you're on crutches.'

'It isn't. And anyway Mrs P doesn't like me messing about in her kitchen. But,' doubtfully, 'would you really do that? For *me*?'

'Why not?' Giana had said briskly. 'I'll make something for both of us.'

The kitchen was at the back of the house, overlooking the now darkened garden. Thus Giana wasn't aware that anyone else had arrived until she heard the sound of voices in the front hall. She froze. Breid was back. And he had someone with him. A woman. A new secretary maybe?

'Oh, Breid, love,' she heard a husky female voice exclaim, 'what an absolute gem of a house.' The endearment knocked the secretary theory on the head.

'I'm glad you like it,' Breid's voice rejoined, 'since you're going to be living here for a long time.'

'Like it! I absolutely love it. I just know we're going to be very happy here.'

It was as if a vast iron hand had taken Giana's heart and was slowly squeezing the life-blood from it. Breid hadn't wasted much time in finding someone else. He'd told Giana she was responsible for bringing him back to life, but another woman was reaping the benefits.

'How about a cup of tea?' the female voice went on. 'Dare I venture into the dragon's den?'

The voices were coming closer. Tea-towel still in hand, Giana looked vainly for somewhere to hide.

The kitchen door opened and two people entered. One was Breid but Giana dared not look at him; one glimpse of his face and she'd be lost. She concentrated her gaze on his companion. She was considerably older than Giana, nearer Breid's own age. She was stylishly and expensively dressed and stunningly attractive with red hair which Giana suspected wasn't entirely natural.

'Heavens! This surely can't be the redoubtable Mrs P?'

'No, Mary won't be back until tomorrow.' Breid's voice cracked on a harsh note as he added, 'This is Mrs Leyburn, Vicky, about whom you've heard so much!'

Vicky? Then this was his sister. Unreasonable relief ran through Giana. Unreasonable because it made no difference to *her* situation.

'Goodness, how fascinating!' Immense blue eyes met Giana's as the woman advanced further into the kitchen. 'I have indeed heard a lot about you.'

'I was just leaving,' Giana observed to a space in mid-air somewhere between the two people confronting her.

'Not until you've explained just what you're doing here,' Breid stated flatly.

That was going to be very difficult now and Giana didn't relish attempting it under the amused gaze of the sophisticated Vicky. She became very absorbed in folding the tea-towel and returning it neatly to its proper place.

'I just happened to be in the area so I called in. I left something behind.' It wasn't altogether a lie. She *had* left something behind—her heart.

'That you did not!' Breid retorted emphatically. 'I personally watched you clear every single possession of yours out of my house. And who gave you leave to use Mary's kitchen?'

At this, Giana's anger fuelled her pride and she looked him straight in the eye.

'There was no one here to ask leave of—except your daughter.'

'Tina? You've seen Tina?' His voice became a low growl of anger. 'That's why you're here, isn't it? You're still acting as your husband's lackey. If you've upset her... She's just come through a very nasty experience.'

That was rich! The daughter he'd left to fend for herself. But Giana was damned if she was going to be drawn into an argument, or offer excuses or explanations. She marched towards the doorway which still seemed dauntingly filled by Breid's tall figure.

'If you'll kindly let me pass,' she demanded frostily, 'I'll leave immediately.'

'That might be rather difficult,' Vicky observed, 'if that little car by the gate is yours. I noticed it in the headlights as we came by; you've got a puncture.'

'Oh, no!' Giana groaned. 'Not another one.' There had been no garage between the site of her first puncture and Dinas Mead.

'You mean you've got no spare tyre?' Breid demanded. He sounded tense and utterly exasperated.

'Don't worry!' Giana snapped. 'I've no intention of causing you any inconvenience. I'll walk down to the inn and use their phone to call a garage.'

'The nearest garage is ten miles away,' Breid said wearily, 'and it's only a small one. It's closed on Sundays. It's a bit late to call anyone out. You'd do better to put up at the Cock and Bull and call the garage tomorrow.'

Only Giana knew it was impossible to get a room at the inn, but she wasn't going to tell Breid so.

'She can't walk back down that lonely lane in the pitch dark,' Vicky objected. 'Breid, you'll run her down in the car, won't you?'

'No!' Giana exclaimed. The thought of being alone with Breid in his car was quite unbearable. Then she said more quietly, 'No, thank you, I prefer to walk. I'm not at all nervous of the dark. Besides I've got a torch in the car.'

'And she's hardly likely to encounter a dangerous maniac in Dinas Mead,' Breid concluded. To Giana's relief he stood aside and allowed her to pass, and it was Vicky who saw her to the front door.

'Are you sure you'll be all right?' she asked Giana. 'I can understand it would be a bit embarrassing for you to have Breid drive you.' Apologetically, 'I'd take you myself but I don't drive.'

Giana was aware that Vicky stood in the front door for some time watching her walk away and she was relieved when a bend in the drive hid her from sight. It was a good thing she'd parked down near the gates, she reflected, for of course she had no intention of going down to the Cock and Bull. It was pointless. She could very well sleep in the car just for one night and make her telephone call from the inn first thing next morning.

Although she'd denied being nervous, Giana locked the car doors from the inside before she settled down.

It wasn't going to be the most comfortable night she'd ever spent, she thought as she wriggled restlessly. The back seat wasn't long enough to stretch out comfortably. Though it was officially spring, the nights were still cold and beside the jeans and sweater she wore she only had a travelling rug with which to cover herself. She had considered leaving the engine running so that the car's heating system would warm her, but the possibility of accidentally asphyxiating herself decided her against that.

Yet even if she'd been in the most luxurious bed in the land she wouldn't have been able to sleep. Miserably she imagined what Breid must have told his sister about her. Thank God Vicky was only his sister and she didn't have to picture the two of them making love. She'd rather liked Vicky. The older woman had evinced far more concern for her than Breid had shown.

Despite the cold and her unhappy imaginings, Giana did doze fitfully and it was from one of these unsatisfactory slumbers that she was rudely awakened. At first she couldn't think what was happening. The little car was rocking violently as though it were a small boat on a storm-tossed sea. Then she heard someone shouting and the light of a torch shone through the rear window dazzling her.

'Unlock these doors and come out of there!' Oh, no, it was Breid. And he sounded absolutely furious. Shakily she obeyed.

'What are you doing out here in the middle of the night?' she asked indignantly.

'That's my question,' he snapped. 'You're the one supplying the answer. What the hell are you playing at, sleeping in my drive?'

'Believe me,' Giana retorted, 'if I could have pushed the car it wouldn't be on your precious property.'

'Keys?' he demanded.

'In my pocket. Why?'

'Hand them over.'

'No! I ... Oh, you brute!'

One large hand held both of hers captive whilst the other ransacked the deep pockets of her jeans, the contact unbearably, unwantedly intimate.

The keys in his possession, he relocked the car, then without a word began to march Giana up the drive.

'Let go of me!'

'No way! You're coming up to the house with me.'

'What are you going to do?' she enquired sarcastically. 'Hand me over to the police for trespassing? What harm was I doing?'

'Why didn't you tell me the inn was full, you silly little fool?'

'How do you know it is?'

'Because Vicky rang through to see if you got there all right.' Vicky had been the one to enquire, not Breid, she thought dully. 'She was worried,' Breid went on. 'She made me come out and look for you.'

They had reached the house by now. As they entered the front door Vicky appeared from the kitchen. A look of relief spread across her attractive face.

'Oh, good, you found her.'

'Yes,' Breid said grimly, 'sleeping in her car.'

'Oh, dear, you must be absolutely frozen. Come into the kitchen. I've got the kettle on just in case. Breid, you make her a drink while I go and make up a bed for her.'

'No!' Giana said. 'It's very kind of you, *Vicky*.' She emphasised the older woman's name to let Breid know she realised the gesture wasn't his. 'But there's no need. I wouldn't dream of stopping here.'

Vicky heaved an exasperated sigh.

'*I'll* make the drink. You go and make up the bed, Breid, while I talk some sense into her. Then perhaps we can all get some sleep.'

'I'm sorry!' When Breid was out of sight and earshot, Giana slumped on to one of the kitchen chairs. 'I didn't mean to be a nuisance. I'd have been perfectly all right in the car.'

Vicky put the back of her hand against Giana's cheek.

'My dear girl,' she said drily, 'your goosebumps have got goosebumps. Now let's have no more of this nonsense. You're sleeping here tonight and that's that. It's been a long day. I've been travelling since the crack of dawn and what with Breid insisting I phoned the Cock and Bull for him and then doing his nut because you were missing... Why ever didn't you tell us the inn was full? We would have...'

'Breid asked you to phone the inn?' Giana interrupted. This was a very different story.

'Well, of course. He's a very caring man. He wouldn't wish harm to his worst enemy.'

And that about summed it up, Giana thought wryly. He didn't even wish *her* harm. She sipped the mug of hot chocolate Vicky thrust into her hands.

'Now,' Vicky said sternly, 'I'm going to bed. I'm dead on my feet. And you're going to be sensible, aren't you, and not do a disappearing act?'

'Don't worry, I'll see to that.' Breid had come back sooner than either of them expected. 'There were several beds already made up. Mary obviously wasn't taking any chances. You're in the room you had before,' he told Giana.

'I...I'll go up then.' She stood, the half-finished drink still in her hand. She didn't want Vicky to leave her alone with Breid, but apparently there was no chance of that.

'Good,' he said and remained in the doorway, obviously waiting for her to precede him.

Giana sidled past him. She hadn't intended to look at him, but something drew her eyes to his face, its grave lines, the hard set of his mouth which had once been so tender on hers. Despite the space between them, Giana was acutely aware of him, unable to control the shiver that raced the length of her spine. Her eyes locked with his, their blue-grey pools of ice. She hadn't intended to speak to him either, but,

'Goodnight,' she murmured.

His mouth curled in a not particularly pleasant way.

'I'll see you to your room.'

'There's no need. I know my way.'

'Nevertheless!'

She was bone weary but she had never mounted the stairs so quickly. Yet he kept pace with her, just one step behind. 'Damn him! Damn him!' she whispered to herself under her breath as she mounted the wide staircase. It was the only way she could hold back the tears that pricked her weary eyes.

At the familiar door she stopped and confronted him. 'We're here. Satisfied?'

'By no means.'

'What are you going to do?' she enquired sarcastically. 'Lock me in, in case I pinch the family silver?'

'Oh, I hardly think that will be necessary. There aren't many places you can run to tonight.' He leaned past her, opened the bedroom door and hastily she backed in. But he followed her and closed the door behind him.

'What are you doing?' she said nervously as he crowded in on her. 'What do you want?'

'Not you, so don't worry!' But he took her chin between a strong finger and thumb. 'I'm curious to know just why you did come here today?' He gave her chin a little jerk. 'What are you and that husband of yours up to this time?'

She parted her lips to tell him Anthony was dead, then decided against it. She just couldn't bear it if Breid lowered himself in her estimation by expressing satisfaction at the death of his *bête noire*.

At her mutinous silence Breid gave a lazy cynical smile.

'No lies ready on the tip of your tongue? You do surprise me, Mrs Leyburn.' She tried to jerk her head away but failed to loosen his grasp. 'But then I suppose I shouldn't be surprised at anything you do.'

'What's that supposed to mean?' she demanded suspiciously.

'It means I should expect anything of a woman who'll give her consent to her husband having an affair,' he said contemptuously, 'a woman who'll do her best to further his unscrupulous behaviour.'

Giana had never behaved in such an undignified fashion in her life. She had always detested physical violence, relying on her sharp wits and tongue to give battle, but lost for words now she saw red and attacked Breid with fists and feet.

'You swine!' she choked. 'You utter swine!'

His hands on her shoulders, he sought to restrain her and with a swift darting sideways movement of her head she bit his wrist and knew, almost before the savage growl he uttered, that she'd gone too far.

His grip became vice-like as he slammed her hard up against his body and glared down into her face, white now with fear at what she saw in his face.

'No,' she said through bloodless lips. 'No, Breid, please. I...'

'Too late for apologies, even if you were thinking of offering one.'

'Well, I wasn't,' she snapped, but it was a feeble snap. She was far too aware of him, of every line of his hard body pressed against hers, of the knowledge that though it might be anger-based he was aroused.

Then his mouth came down on hers, forcing it open in a kiss that held no tenderness. It was a savage assault and Giana whimpered protestingly as she felt his teeth draw blood from her lower lip.

'An eye for an eye, a tooth for a tooth, a bite for a bite,' he muttered. But his voice was husky, thickened. 'What other return shall I make to you for what you've done to me?'

Very quietly, she said, 'I hate you.'

'Do you?' He was smiling but there was a sneer in his voice that angered her. 'Face it, Giana, you want me as much as you hate me. Hate me all you like,' he went on, 'but you owe me, Giana Leyburn.'

'I owe you nothing,' she cried desperately as he swung her up in his arms and carried her towards the bed.

'No? What about this?' He threw her down and came down half on top of her, his weight imprisoning her so that she was unable to move as his face bent to hers once more and he took possession again of her trembling lips. 'And this,' he muttered fiercely against the hollow at the base of her throat as his hard seeking fingers kneaded her breasts.

He was right of course. She did want him. She only had to be in the same room as him and her body flamed into awareness. And now, crushed in his arms, she was overcome with a painful need.

'I'm going to have you, Giana,' he stated. 'You were thrown at me, bait for a trap. I've evaded the trap but I'm still going to have the bait. Such a tasty bait!'

'Breid, no! You're acting out of character,' she told him desperately. 'You're not that sort of person. You'll regret it afterwards.'

'Maybe, but right at this moment that doesn't seem to matter very much.' He pulled her into him so that once again she felt the hard aroused tension of his body. Roughly, despite her struggles, he yanked off her pullover, his eyes going hungrily to the straining breasts covered only by the flimsiest of bras which did not long detain his urgent hands. Then his mouth on her breasts was hot and seeking, his tongue leaving a trail of moisture around the aroused nipples.

At first Giana continued to fight but as his kisses, his caresses grew more intense, she gasped both with pain and desire. His potent masculine odour brought primitive shudders of delight to her body until at last all thoughts of resistance had fled and she kissed him back with all her strength. All she wanted was to know the tensile pleasure of bone, muscle and flesh as her hands slipped beneath his shirt to caress him and pull him closer. She shuddered and urged her hips against him as his hand sought the waistband of her jeans. She made no protest as he stripped them from her. Instead she unfastened the buckle of his belt and set out on her own voyage of exploration.

He raised himself for an instant to facilitate the movement of her hands, looking down on her with eyes that had turned from cold grey-blue to a dark intensity.

'God,' he muttered thickly, 'but you're exquisite.' Then his hands and his mouth were wooing her subtly along the path he meant them to take. He dealt with her only remaining garment, his hands brushing against the flat silken planes of her stomach.

Her body jerked spasmodically as he continued his exploration, his breathing harsh and painful, telling her with what difficulty he held himself in check. Why was he holding back? There was no need, her lips and her caresses told him.

'So eager, Giana?' he enquired softly.

'Oh, yes, yes, Breid.' Eyes closed, aware only of feeling, her body urged him to take her. She reached out for him, urgent to touch and to know his manhood.

'Oh, no, you don't.'

Bewildered hazel eyes, slumbrous with desire, opened and she looked up into his passion-darkened face, not comprehending.

'Oh, no, Giana.' He thrust himself away from her. 'That's all you're getting from me. By the look in your eyes, the story of your body tells me, I'm sufficiently revenged. You want me. How you want me! Well, you can go on wanting.'

The warm, honeyed longing dissolved into pain, then anger, as she stared into his taut cold face.

'You deliberately...?'

'Yes.' He stood up adjusting his clothing. 'Good-night, *Mrs Leyburn*,' he said tauntingly. 'I hope it *won't* be.'

CHAPTER EIGHT

'GOOD morning. I hope you like tea in bed? Some people can't stand it.'

Giana struggled up out of a bottomless well of unrefreshing sleep to see Vicky sitting on the side of her bed proffering a cup.

'You shouldn't have,' she protested as she accepted the drink. 'Have I overslept?'

'That rather depends on whether you're one of the world's workers or one of its drones,' Vicky said wryly. 'Me, I'm a devout drone when I'm allowed to be and I call this early. It's nine o'clock.'

'That's late!' Giana exclaimed. 'I meant to be up long ago. I want to get away.'

'Before you could encounter my brother again, I imagine?' The cup wobbled dangerously and tea overflowed into the saucer. 'A lot of things have become very clear to me this morning,' Vicky went on, 'and to Breid, too, come to that. Just as well I'm here, if you ask me.'

Giana took a long sip of the tea.

'I'm sorry,' she apologised, 'but I seem to be a bit muddle-headed this morning. I must have slept too heavily.' Which wasn't surprising, she thought, since she'd cried herself to sleep last night. 'Why *are* you here? I thought you lived in the South of France.'

'That's me! Ten out of ten! My husband's firm have given him a transfer back to the UK, but as they're always moving him around we decided not to buy a house but to rent this one from Breid. I'm the advance party. The rest of the family will arrive next week.'

'So Breid won't be living here any more?'

Vicky grimaced.

'Not, if he's got any sense, with us and our brood— we have four children—not an ideal setting in which to write books. I'm also taking on Breid's main problem . . . Tina. He thinks I may have more influence with her than he has. So it'll be a full house.' She was silent for a while, tracing the pattern on the bedcover. 'And speaking of Tina, you seem to have had quite an effect on her yourself.'

'Oh?' Giana said warily. 'In what way?'

'It seems she had quite a little heart to heart with Breid this morning.' Vicky pulled another face. 'About dawn apparently. Which is why I was dragged out of bed around seven o'clock to listen to him. Tina has, as they say, spilled the beans.'

'She has?' Giana's heart began to beat suffocatingly fast.

'Yes, and now Breid knows exactly why you came to Dinas Mead in the first place and why you're here this time.' Slowly, 'He also knows that your husband is dead.' Vicky looked at Giana sharply. 'Do I commiserate or not?'

'I wouldn't have wished him dead,' Giana said simply.

'And how do you feel about my brother?' And, as Giana flushed scarlet, 'OK, don't answer that one either. Your face speaks for itself. The one who isn't too sure about it is Breid himself.'

'I shouldn't think he'd care. He can't stand the sight of me,' Giana retorted. 'When he found out who I was he couldn't wait to get me out of his house. And you saw the way he acted last night.' Her colour deepened as she recalled that Vicky could have no idea of some of her brother's behaviour.

'I also saw the way he acted this morning, after Tina's revelations. Right at this moment I should say my brother is a very mixed-up man.'

Not half as mixed up as she was, Giana thought. Vicky's words had implanted a tiny seed of hope in her heart but she feared to let it grow.

'After my sister-in-law was killed he never got around to building a new life,' Vicky went on, 'nor to meeting people again, especially women. He became virtually a recluse.'

'I know,' Giana said. The image of Breid's haunted features as he'd told her of Francesca's death was still disturbingly vivid, still awakened that ache within her, the longing to comfort him with every means at her disposal.

'He shut himself away and began writing more and more, because he was so filled with despair and anger that it was suffocating him. And I suppose that seemed the best way of dealing with it. He seemed to find it easier to write than to talk. And yet,' Vicky looked at Giana assessingly, 'it seems he's talked to you about it.'

'That's the awful part,' Giana confessed. 'That he trusted me and all the time I was deceiving him. No wonder he hates me.' But he need not have taken hatred so far, she thought unhappily.

'Oh I don't think he hates you, Giana, far from it. Things would be much less complicated if he did. Personally I think he's in love with you.'

'No.' Giana shook her head very positively.

'Oh, yes,' Vicky insisted. 'Even before I met you I thought that, even when we both still thought you were working with your husband. Underneath the anger there was some other strong emotion.'

'I'd have to hear it from his own lips before I'd believe it,' Giana was ironic.

'That's the difficulty,' Vicky said. And, as Giana looked at her uncomprehendingly, 'Breid hasn't got many faults, though I dare say as his sister I'm prejudiced. But one thing he does seem to have suffered from since Francesca died is a kind of diffidence where women are concerned.'

'Diffidence?' That was a good one after last night.

'Yes, Giana. How are you on faults? Would you say one of your faults was pride?'

Giana thought about it. Looking back over the recent weeks she didn't feel as though pride had played much of a part in her relationship with Breid.

'I don't think so,' she said warily, 'but it's difficult to judge your own faults.'

'You'll soon know,' Vicky told her, 'because if this situation is going to be straightened out, you're the one who's going to have to do it.'

'How?' Giana was aghast, not from affronted pride but from the fear of further rejection. It was all very well for Vicky to have theories. *She* wasn't the one who was going to have to test them.

'For a start you're going to have to find him.'

'Breid's disappeared?' If Vicky had any doubts about Giana's feelings for Breid, her anguished expression would have settled them.

'Well, not off the face of the earth exactly,' she said reassuringly. 'But he's gone to ground. I think he's bit-

terly ashamed of the way he's treated you, and I don't
think he's expecting forgiveness or that you could pos-
sibly have any feelings left for him. Among his virtues,'
she added, 'he does number modesty.'

'But he's the one who ought to be forgiving me!' Giana
insisted hotly. 'He had every right to be furious with me.
I gave him a false name, worked for him under false
pretences.' She groaned. 'The list is endless. We'd need
an umpire, not a matchmaker.'

'After last night I make the score about deuce,' Vicky
said with a grin. 'But I still reckon if you could find him
and let him see just how you feel it'd be game set and
match to you. How about it, Giana? Will you try?'

There had only been one possible answer to that, Giana
thought as she drove away from Dinas Mead late that
afternoon, after several frustrating hours getting her
punctured tyres fixed. If there was any chance that Vicky
was right about her brother's feelings, Giana had to take
it.

She couldn't be certain she was taking the right
direction as she set off into the East Anglian countryside,
but there was a fair chance that Breid had gone back to
the Broads.

Her progress seemed frustratingly slow. Once Giana
had decided on a course of action she was not one to
hang back from it. She desperately wanted to see Breid
and end the torturing suspense. Sheer fatigue made her
stop once or twice for a rest, but, at last, in the growing
dusk, she saw the signs for Ulfketle.

Over the bridge beyond the Fisherman's Return the
fields were visible, no longer covered in flood water, and
slowly moving cows appreciated its verdant greens.

Then the car was bumping over the bridge by the lock and in the distance she could see the sturdy white walls of The Retreat. Her heart gave a skip, half joy, half fear. Parked on the hardstand was Breid's Rolls.

The door wasn't locked. Both here and at Foxdene she'd noted this lack of security consciousness. Perhaps knowing that a determined burglar would overcome all barriers, Breid had adopted an attitude of fatality. Or maybe he just suffered from writer's absent-mindedness.

She made her way through the empty lounge and looked through the door that led into the ground-floor extension. Several cardboard boxes piled with groceries stood on the kitchen worktop. Judging by their contents Breid was preparing for a long stay. A sound from behind her made her whirl on her heel. Breid stood at the bottom of the stairs. He seemed to loom very large. Giana summoned up all her courage.

'Hello, Breid,' she said quietly. Her hazel eyes devoured the familiar beloved features, searching for some sign of welcome, but at that moment his face showed only fatigue. It drew almost immediately into pugnacious lines, the well-shaped mouth hard with annoyance.

'This seems to be becoming a habit with you, Mrs Leyburn,' he said, 'walking unannounced and uninvited into my home.'

'I know it must seem an intrusion,' she agreed with him would-be-placatingly, 'but I felt I ought to come.'

'Why?' Whatever his feelings for her, he certainly wasn't going to give her any help.

Giana swallowed.

'Because, although you know the truth about me now...'

'I know the truth, do I?' There was bitterness in his voice but he had control of his expression now. It was bleak and shuttered, his handsome features as cold and hard as when they'd first met. 'What is the truth? I don't know and I'm not sure you do.'

'Because,' she persevered, 'there are an awful lot of loose ends that need tying up. For one thing, I owe you an apology.'

'You could have written.'

Giana shook her head. 'To me that seems the cowardly way out. I've always believed an apology should be made face to face.'

He shrugged. 'Your apology is accepted.' There was no warmth in him whatsoever, no emotion, not even anger now, and Giana suddenly exploded, all her good resolutions forgotten.

'Is that it?' she demanded. 'So what am I supposed to do now? Turn round and drive all the way back to London?'

'I'm not a mind-reader,' he drawled. 'What else do you want here? What were you planning to do?' There was something unnatural about his control, his indifferent manner.

'That rather depended on you,' she told him.

'Why?' he asked sarcastically. 'Were you hoping I'd invite you to stay?'

'Yes,' she said explosively, 'I was. I was also hoping you might have the grace to say something to me as well.' This outburst elicited only a raised eyebrow. 'Don't you think,' she went on desperately, 'that you ought to apologise, too, to me? For all the accusations you made, the insinuations that I was working with my husband, against you. For...' She'd been about to say 'for last night', but he interrupted her.

'Weren't you working with him?'

'No, I damn well was not. I hated his methods just as much as you did. You even insinuated that I was condoning his relationship with Tina.'

'I realise that at least isn't true,' he admitted.

'Good! Well for those reasons at least you owe me an apology.'

'Would it do any good? If I apologised for those reasons...and more?' There was a strange note of intensity in his tone.

'You could always try and find out,' she told him.

'Very well then, I apologise. I admit I misunderstood your motives...at least some of them.'

'And what exactly does that mean?' she enquired suspiciously.

'No, let me ask you something instead.' There was a little more colour to his voice and Giana waited tensely. 'Just how much of your behaviour was directed towards finding out why I was interested in your husband?' Bright angry colour ran up in Giana's cheeks but she wasn't given a chance to expostulate as he went on, 'No, hear me out. I'm not reneging on my apology. But you backed off, didn't you? Why did you even let things go that far if you didn't intend to go any further? Was there any other reason?'

This was one of those moments when pride must not be allowed to get the upper hand.

'You mean,' Giana said bluntly, 'why did I let you make love to me and then refuse to...to go all the way? At that time,' she told him, 'as far as I was concerned

I was still a married woman. I wasn't free to...to do what I wanted to do.'

'You *wanted* me to make love to you?' Was there a suspicion of unsteadiness in his voice now?

Without some encouragement pride could only be debased just so far, Giana was finding. She became evasive.

'I think you know that answer to that.'

'No!' exasperatedly, 'I don't know. I'm not even sure why you're here now if all you wanted was a mere exchange of politenesses. Damn it,' he complained wearily, 'why are we standing here like a couple of sparring partners? For God's sake let's sit down somewhere.'

Giana was glad to do so. The tiring drive and the effort of confronting him were combining to make her legs dangerously weak. She chose the couch and after a moment's hesitation he joined her but kept his distance. Even so she was intensely aware of him.

'All right,' she said, her voice tremulous, 'I didn't come here just to apologise, or to hear you apologise. I wanted to help you to...'

'Help me!' He didn't let her finish. 'I know now of course that you're no secretary. You're a trained nurse, a professional do-gooder. Do you see this as some extension of your job?' He was ironic. 'Have you come here to try and rehabilitate me?'

'No!' This was emotionally exhausting. She seemed to be getting nowhere and acute depression gripped her. 'I...'

'Of course counselling the bereaved would be part of your training, wouldn't it?' White lines of anger were drawn from the nostrils of his finely shaped nose to the corners of his mouth. 'And you came down to Dinas

Mead this last time thinking you'd have to break the news of my daughter's death.'

'Yes,' she choked on the admission, 'but . . .'

'Experience in the field, was it?'

'No!' The unfairness brought the threatening tears closer to the surface.

'Because you felt it was your duty?'

'No.' Her hazel eyes were overbright now. 'I . . .'

'Tears, Giana? Was it because you pitied me? Damn it, Giana, I don't want your *pity*.'

'Shut up!' she cried. 'Stop taking everything the wrong way. Just shut up and listen for a change. It's true I came to Foxdene to tell you what I thought had happened to Tina. But I came,' she said passionately, 'because I couldn't bear the thought of you hearing it from a stranger, the thought of your unhappiness. You've had so much tragedy in your life.'

'So what made you think hearing it from you might soften the blow?'

'Because, damn you,' she was sobbing openly now, unable to see his face through the mist of tears, 'because I love you and I thought *you* loved *me*!' She had lost all inhibitions, all fear of consequences. To hell with pride.

'Aaah.' It was a throaty purr. '*That's* what I've been waiting to hear.'

'Oh, have you!' she hiccuped. 'Did it never occur to you that I might be waiting to hear you say something like that?'

'Frankly, no,' he said soberly. 'I couldn't be sure that you weren't still in love with your husband, in spite of everything that's happened. Oh, don't cry, my little love.' He moved closer and took her in his arms. Beneath her cheek his chest rose and fell in a great sigh as if some weight had been lifted from him. 'Giana, can you ever forgive me for the way I behaved last night? Darling, I punished myself as much as I hurt you. I didn't get a moment's sleep all night.'

'Of... of course I forgive you,' she hiccuped. 'But it did hurt, dreadfully.'

'I think we understand each other now. It's all over now,' he soothed, as she continued to sob, 'bar the shouting.'

'Bar the shouting!' It was half a sob, half a laugh against his chest. 'I thought that was all we'd been doing, shouting at each other.'

'We'll never shout at each other again,' he vowed as he wiped her eyes.

'Goodness,' Giana was recovering fast, little bubbles of happiness beginning to well up inside her like a spring, 'don't expect me to make promises like that. We're both of us far too human to live like saints.'

'Now that I can endorse!' His tone was wicked now. 'I've lived a celibate ascetic life far too long.' He peered into her face. 'Do you think we might do something about that?'

'Right now?' Giana teased, though she made no attempt to move from the comforting circle of his arms. 'When I'm starving?'

'Do you know,' he sounded surprised, 'so am I? I left Foxdene without stopping for breakfast and I haven't eaten since.' Gravely, 'How about an early supper?'

'And then what?' Her hazel eyes studied his beloved face.

'Whatever you like, my love.' He was tender. 'We never did have that period of getting to know each other, did we? If you want that old-fashioned courtship I promised you...'

Giana's smile sparkled lovingly up at him.

'That would be very nice,' she said demurely. And, at his swiftly concealed look of disappointment, 'Would an hour or so after supper be long enough for a courtship, do you think?'

'Far too long!' he responded instantly, attuned at once to her mood. 'But I'll allow it. I plan to be an indulgent husband... very indulgent,' he growled mock fiercely against her neck. Then, hugging her, 'Oh, Giana, it seems the only time I can really laugh is when I'm with you.'

She lifted her hand and touched his face. It was such happiness to be able to touch and to look at him again without fear, to know that there were no restraints to the expression of their love. Her face was alight with love and longing.

'Oh, Breid...' Her breath mingled with his as he bent his head to kiss her. It was only a light, exploratory kiss but it aroused a yearning response within her and her lips parted eagerly.

Encouraged, he buried his mouth in hers, kissing her with mounting passion, his mouth open-lipped, sensual. His hands captured her face, his thumbs sensuously caressing her cheeks, and a hot tide seemed to rise and engulf them.

She had never known there were so many ways of kissing, to be kissed. He kissed her languorously so that tremors shuddered through her body. He explored her mouth passionately, searching its depths. He kissed her hungrily, a kiss that told of his urgent, aching need for her.

As she groaned her own reaction, longing for him shuddered through her and his hands moved to cover and hold the fullness of her breasts. At once her nipples were erect living things against his circling palms. The lines of her body moulded with his, urged against its hardness.

She wound her fingers into the thick blond hair, re-learning the shape of his head and neck that she'd thought never to know so intimately again.

He raised his head for an instant to look deeply into her eyes.

'Giana, I *did* ask you to marry me?' he enquired throatily.

'Yes.'

'Good,' he sighed in mock relief, 'because that makes the way I feel now almost decent.'

She chuckled appreciatively.

'But it was a long time ago, not recently. I'm not sure that counts.'

'Did I go down on my knees?' he enquired.

'No.'

'Would you like me to ask you properly, now?'

'Don't you dare,' she told him. 'I should get the giggles. And this is no laughing matter. Oh, Breid,' she whispered, suddenly shaken by emotion, 'I want you so much. I've never wanted anything or anyone as much as I want you.'

'What happened to that period of courtship?' he teased, but his voice was as husky and unsteady as hers.

'We have the rest of our lives for that.' Her eyes were wanton with desire. 'Our lives will be one long courtship.'

'True, but it would be very unromantic if my stomach were to rumble,' he suggested. He hadn't pulled away from her but she sensed a slight withdrawal in him. Maybe it was Breid who wanted to keep this thing light-hearted for the moment. Maybe he didn't want things to go too fast. Perhaps even now the past still had its hold on him. Perhaps he was still afraid of making the final commitment. Giana tempered her mood to his.

'Very unromantic,' she agreed. Gently, she freed herself from his embrace and stood up. 'So let's see what you've brought in those cardboard boxes,' she suggested. 'Did you raid Mary Pimblett's store cupboards, or what?'

'Or what, of course,' he told her. 'I went to a supermarket in Ipswich.' In mock horror, 'It'd be more than my life was worth for Mary to find her cupboards bare.'

'Vicky says you're letting Foxdene to her,' Giana said as together they prepared a meal. 'And that you're moving out. Are you going to work at the London house?'

'Some of the time maybe. But a lot of the time I plan to be here, unless you've any strong objections?'

'None whatsoever,' she assured him earnestly. 'I love this place.'

'What about your job?'

'I should have to give that up, I suppose.'

'Would that matter very much?'

'I've enjoyed my work but I'm a little tired of trying to care for everyone.' She added lightly, 'I'd sooner devote my attentions to one particular person.'

They kept the mood light-hearted throughout their meal and during the washing up, at which Breid insisted on assisting.

'I can still hardly believe you're here, so I certainly don't intend to let you out of my sight,' he said, when Giana suggested he go and sit down.

'I'm not used to having a man in the kitchen,' she told him. Anthony had never helped around the flat.

'Then you'd better get used to it.'

'I find it very disturbing,' she told him, openly flirting with him. But he merely smiled and, a little deflated, she returned her attention to the dishes. Maybe it wasn't going to be so easy after all to lift the shadows away from his life.

When they returned to the living-room Giana deliberately chose to sit in a chair. She didn't want to force the pace. Breid knew how she felt. It was up to him now.

He seemed restless, prowling the large apartment, picking things up, putting them down.

'Do you mind if we talk for a bit?' he asked abruptly.

'Of course not,' she said immediately. If he still had things on his mind it would be better for him to talk them out.

'Did Vicky tell you I'd asked her to look after Tina? I don't want you to think you're going to be landed with a difficult stepdaughter.'

'She told me. But I wouldn't have minded. You would have found it very hard,' she ventured to joke, 'to put me off you.' But he went on seriously.

'I feel I must warn you, I don't know that I could bear to start another family. To risk the heartbreak. I feel I've failed Tina somewhere along the way.' He stopped his pacing for a moment to look at her. 'Giana, have you any conception of the terrible remorse parents sometimes feel, the sense of failure and the impotence of not being able to put things right?' He resumed his pacing but was silent for so long that Giana felt something was demanded of her.

'If you're asking me whether I mind not having children,' she said, 'the answer is that I want whatever you want.'

He paused again to look at her doubtfully.

'You'd be content just to build your life around one man, one rather selfish man. For I am selfish, Giana. Writers are selfish people. Do you realise what I'm saying? In effect I'm saying I want you all to myself and yet there are times when I shall forget you're there. Times when I'll be brusque and impatient because you've interrupted my train of thought. If you had children...'

'If I had children,' she interrupted, 'it would only be because you wanted them, too. As to building my life around you, I've wanted nothing else almost from the first moment I saw you.'

'You make me feel very humble,' he said quietly.

She got up and went to him then.

'I don't want you to feel humble,' she told him, her hand on his arm. 'I want you to be proud, as I shall be proud of our love, of your loving me.' Her heart was beating with a breathless urgency. She wanted him to throw aside all his doubts and anxieties. She wanted him to kiss her. She wanted it with a burning need. But she waited. Somehow she knew it was important to wait.

He gave a sudden exclamation that was almost a groan and pulled her to him, his body hardening immediately. She was conscious of a hundred tense muscles, of the shudders that went through him. Against her soft breasts his heart thudded and she could hear his hard breathing. With gentle fingers she kneaded his shoulders, the tight muscles of his neck, and gradually she felt him relax.

Slowly she drew him toward the couch and pulled him down beside her.

'Is there anything else worrying you?' she asked him gently as his arm circled her shoulders.

His smile was an ineffably weary one.

'Careful, Giana, the professional manner's showing through again. No, no,' as her lips parted in indignant protest, 'I'm only teasing, love. I'm grateful for your understanding. If only I'd met you years ago. What a lot of time has been wasted.'

'We'll make up for it.' She nestled against him, undemanding, content to comfort him merely by her presence.

He yawned, suddenly, deeply.

'God, Giana, I'm tired. I feel as if all the tiredness of the last few years has finally caught up with me. I feel as though I could sleep for a month.' His arm about her tightened. 'Which is a very unflattering thing to say to the woman you love.'

'Not at all,' she told him. 'I shan't be offended if you go to sleep. So long as I'm the one sleeping with you.'

He turned his head against her hair in an effort to see her face.

'I believe you really mean that. Will you share my bed tonight, Giana?'

'Yes.'

He stood, taking her with him. Arms wrapped about each other they negotiated the winding stairs, right to the very top, to his room. They were both tired now and it was uncertain who was supporting whom.

Breid sat on the edge of the bed and made a half-hearted attempt to unlace his shoes. Then with a sigh he rolled back and sideways, drawing his legs up on to the bed. His eyes closed. In another moment, Giana knew he would be asleep, so total was his exhaustion. It wasn't just physical, she suspected. He had been under an emotional strain for far too long.

Carefully, so as not to disturb him, she removed his shoes. A search in an ottoman revealed spare bedding and a blanket. The blanket she threw over him, then, stripping down until only her undies remained, she crept under it beside him, close enough for him to feel the reassurance of her presence. Then she, too, slept.

When she woke again it was still dark. The luminous dial of her watch showed that she had only been asleep for a couple of hours. At first she couldn't think what had disturbed her. Then she realised. She was alone on the big bed. She sat up, alarmed.

'Breid?'

'It's all right.' His voice came to her from the adjoining bathroom. 'Sorry I woke you. I stubbed my toe in the dark. I was trying to undress without disturbing you.' He was a darker shadow against shadows as he came back to bed and lay down only inches away. He didn't touch her but awareness lay between them, a much desired third in their company.

'Breid?' she whispered his name. 'Are you still tired?'

'No.' The uneven way he was breathing made her catch her own breath.

'Neither am I.'

He turned towards her and then there was no gap. He was completely naked and she could feel the trembling in him.

'Giana,' his voice was a mere breath on her face. 'I want to make love to you...desperately. Do you think we could dispense with that courtship period?'

Her breath caught in her throat and for a moment she couldn't speak. Breid snapped on the overhead light and looked anxiously into her face.

'I can't think of anything I'd like more.' She moved against him invitingly.

She clung to his shoulders as he kissed her, as his feverish lips explored not only her mouth, but her throat, plundering its hollows. He removed her bra so that his head could move downward and his tongue could manipulate her nipples, drawing erotic whirls around them, making her breasts throb and ache. He trapped a thrusting tip between his teeth, tugging softly but insistently, while his hands stroked over her body.

She released the long, tormenting moan of need that had built up inside her, twisting and arching against him in passionate frenzy, wanting him to take her.

'Touch me, Giana,' he muttered feverishly against her lips. 'For God's sake, touch me.'

His naked body was smooth and warm. She let her hands slide round to his back, exploring the line of his spine, the taut muscles of his back, his buttocks.

'Go on,' he whispered hoarsely until, becoming bolder, her fingers caressed the hard maleness of him.

Delicate shudders of reaction whispered through her as he in turn explored her femininity. Somehow—she did not notice its going—her only garment was removed.

'Oh, my God,' he whispered as she made no protest when his intimate touch extended its field with hands that shook. It was as if this last submission broke down all his reserve. 'Giana, yours is the first tenderness I've known for years. The sweetness of it overwhelms me.' There was a ragged note in his voice that caught at her heart.

She opened her eyes to see his face rigid with an intolerable hunger.

'Love me, Breid,' she cried aloud. 'Love me.'

He took her then with no further preamble, the driving thrust of his body totally out of control. Exquisite sensations racked her making her dizzy as together their bodies strained towards the much needed fulfilment. And at last it came in a wave of unbelievable pleasure and in the midst of her own ecstasy she heard Breid cry out, a sound that was one of joy, triumph, anguish all mingled. She felt his tears upon her face and held him to her while three years of pent-up frustration flooded from him like water from a burst dam.

He lay in her arms like one dead for a long, long while, his lean body totally collapsed in the exhaustion of utter satisfaction. When at last he lifted his head, the masculine firmness of his features had changed to a clear and soft reflection of profound feeling.

'I love you,' he whispered.

'And I love you.' She was almost shy now that the heights had been scaled. But she believed him and knew that never again would either of them have to question why. The answer to all of life and love was theirs irrevocably.

IS PASSION A CRIME?

HOT ICE *by Nora Roberts* £2.95

A reckless, beautiful, wealthy woman and a professional thief. Red hot passion meets cold hard cash and it all adds up to a sizzling novel of romantic suspense.

GAMES *by Irma Walker* £2.50
(Best selling author of Airforce Wives under the name of Ruth Walker)

Tori Cockran is forced to save her son by the same means that destroyed her marriage and her father — gambling. But first she must prove to the casino boss she loves that she's not a liar and a cheat.

SEASONS OF ENCHANTMENT *by Casey Douglas* £2.75

Ten years after their broken marriage and the loss of their baby, can Beth and Marsh risk a second chance at love? Or will their differences in background still be a barrier?

All available from February 1989.

W●RLDWIDE

From: Boots, Martins, John Menzies, W H Smith, Woolworths and other paperback stockists.

STORIES OF PASSION AND ROMANCE SPANNING FIVE CENTURIES.

CLAIM THE CROWN – *Carla Neggers* _____ £2.95
When Ashley Wakefield and her twin brother inherit a trust fund, they are swept into a whirlwind of intrigue, suspense, danger and romance. Past events unfold when a photograph appears of Ashley wearing her magnificent gems.

JASMINE ON THE WIND – *Mallory Dorn Hart* _____ £3.50
The destinies of two young lovers, separated by the tides of war, merge in this magnificent Saga of romance and high adventure set against the backdrop of dazzling Medieval Spain.

A TIME TO LOVE – *Jocelyn Haley* _____ £2.50
Jessica Brogan's predictable, staid life is turned upside down when she rescues a small boy from kidnappers. Should she encourage the attentions of the child's gorgeous father, or is he simply acting through a sense of gratitude?

These three new titles will be out in bookshops from January 1989.

W●RLDWIDE

Available from Boots, Martins, John Menzies, WH Smith, Woolworths and other paperback stockists.